WATCH ME

SHAYLA BLACK

ABOUT THIS BOOK

To achieve her dreams, all she has to do is seduce the enemy...

Shanna York was set to achieve her glittering ballroom dreams and become a dance champion—until her dance partner gets tangled up in scandal and blackmail. With the clock ticking and all her ambitions at stake, the last thing she needs is the gorgeous owner of a sex club tempting her with the forbidden. Or maybe that's the very thing she needs...

Alejandro Diaz has sizzled for Shanna since he set eyes on her months ago. Her repeated rebuffs will make her surrender that much sweeter. She's ambitious and driven...but so is he. When she asks for his assistance to ensnare a voyeuristic blackmailer with a video fetish, he doesn't hesitate to help her stage a bedroom trap. But neither is prepared to face scorching, endless passion, the blackmailer's real identity—or the undeniable love that grows between them.

WATCH ME

Written by Shayla Black

This book is an original publication by Shayla Black.

Copyright © 2007 Shelley Bradley LLC

Cover Design by: Rachel Connolly

Print ISBN 978-1-936596-57-7

1

*W*ho'd known it would only take two minutes, seventeen seconds to ruin her life?

Shanna York ejected the flash drive from her laptop, resisting the pointless urge to fling it across the room. Instead, she set it gently on the table beside her and stood.

Damn Kristoff! What *had* he been thinking?

Besides looking for inventive ways to get off, absolutely nothing. That was obvious.

Any hope of the life she'd worked and sweated for was over. Goodbye, California Dance Star competition, which she and Kristoff were favored to win in eight days. *Adios*, any chance of making World Cup Latin finals—something she'd been striving for her entire dance career.

Kristoff knew how important this season was to her. *Knew* it. She was twenty-eight—old by ballroom standards. He was the best partner she'd ever had, which was saying something. This year was their year; everyone said so.

All it had taken was one piece of footage recorded just last week —according to the date in the lower right corner of the screen—and a note with a scrawled *Watch Me* to shatter her dreams.

Sighing, Shanna closed her eyes and tried to think. But that only focused the drive's every image into full Technicolor in her memory. Kristoff, tall and ungodly handsome, standing above two figures, one male, the other female. He cradled each of their heads in his hands as they knelt before him. Their tongues slid up and down his erection, licked over his balls, and occasionally met at the head of his cock for a juicy kiss.

"You like that big dick?" he asked. They both moaned. The camera zoomed in as the woman, a stunning blonde with a starburst tattoo on her breast, deep-throated Kristoff.

The other male, a buff guy with military short hair and his own raging hard-on, stood and licked at Kristoff's nipples. Kristoff groaned, the sound soon drowned out by the man capturing his lips and devouring them in a harsh kiss.

That was the first thirty seconds—plenty depraved by the deeply traditional standards many ballroom judges held. Then came the middle of the clip...

Kristoff, intent and focused as he penetrated the woman's sex, plunging in for slow, agonizing strokes. A surprise, given the fact Shanna had always believed he was strictly gay. But thrusting into the woman, he appeared like any other hetero man...until the camera panned back and showed the other man penetrating Kristoff's ass, the forward momentum of that stroke pushing Kristoff's erection into the panting female.

The end of the video, however, was what Shanna feared could really kill her dreams of being a ballroom champion. The other man, apparently at the end of his restraint, tore off his condom and stood near the woman's sex as Kristoff so diligently pounded it. The man with dark hair watched them, yanking on his cock until semen shot out, coating the woman's clit and wet folds. They all groaned.

Kristoff quickly pulled out of her, tugged on his erection, and came on the woman's swollen sex, too. She dripped semen, oozed with the fluids of the men's satisfaction. Was that enough for Kristoff? Of course not.

He grabbed the other man's shoulders and forced him to kneel before the woman's dripping sex beside him. Together, they licked her. Clean. Deep. Until she orgasmed against their dueling tongues. During the clip's final moments, the camera panned back again to reveal that the trio had performed the entire scene for a rapt audience.

Shanna put her head in her hands and groaned. She was so screwed. If the conservative judges of ever-elegant ballroom dance got hold of this footage... The thought of what they could—and would—do to hers and Kristoff's scores at the California Dance Star made her shudder. Nothing like going from first to worst in the standings.

Equally unnerving, watching the scene had more than vaguely aroused Shanna. Not that she was attracted to Kristoff—and definitely not after the position he'd put her in with this stunt. But the freedom to just let loose and fulfill her fantasies, particularly with people watching, flipped her switch way more than it should.

That had to stop. She must deal with the situation, somehow ensure this video didn't fall into the judges' hands. She must not think about her neglected libido.

Where was Kristoff, damn it? He had to have known that his recent jaunts to that damn sex club, *Sneak Peek*, would eventually come back to haunt them. She'd warned him. Clearly, he hadn't heeded a word.

The door of her small dressing room burst open. Kristoff glided in. The graceful bastard moved like glass, especially on the dance floor, which was a treat after living with her father and three brothers: an Olympic sprinter, a world-class decathlete, a former champion weightlifter, and a pro football player, respectively.

They all considered her a failure because she'd never been a champion. By their definition, ballroom dancing wasn't even a sport. Which made her a double loser.

This year, she'd intended to show them different.

With Kristoff's night at that crazy sex club for exhibitionists and voyeurs, her dreams were gone.

"Three minutes, Shan. Are you ready?" Kristoff held out his hand to her.

Normally, that was Shanna's cue to take it and follow his lead. Not tonight.

"To kill you, yes!" She held up the flash drive. "Obviously, your brain sunk into your pants. Could you not have waited to get your jollies for another few weeks?"

He frowned, looking totally unamused. "What do you talk of?"

"Your recent threesome at that club."

Kristoff's polished smile faded. "I was just, um, how do you say, blowing off a little steam. How did you know?"

"Someone filmed you and sent me the footage. Full color, high quality, great sound. No question it's you, near a sign that said *Sneak Peek*."

"Filmed me... I had no idea. And someone sent it to you?" he croaked. "You saw it?"

"Yes, along with a little note informing me that if we show up to the California Star, they'll distribute the clip to all the judges. And you know what will happen then. We'll have no chance in hell of winning."

He cursed, a popular Angelo-Saxon syllable that started with an F. Shanna shook her head. He'd already done that, thanks so much.

"I agreed to take you as my partner for two reasons: You're an amazing dancer, and I thought you were discreetly gay. Gay, the judges can handle. Discreetly gay, even better. Clearly, I was wrong about your orientation. And if the judges see this, your talent will no longer matter to them."

Kristoff flushed. "I am, um...equal opportunity when it comes to sex."

"I gathered that." She gritted her teeth. "And it's fine. I don't care what you do in your private life as long as it's *private*."

"One minute!" someone shouted from the hall.

Squatting, Shanna peered into the mirror at her dressing table, secured a pin holding back a lock of her pale blond hair, then smoothed a hand down the silver sequins of her tiny costume. God, she felt sick to her stomach. All the years of sacrifice and work... If she wanted to win—and she did—she was probably going to have to start over. New season...new partner. Even the thought made her sick. She hoped her tumult didn't show on her face.

"We have to go," she said. "Or we'll be late."

"Stop! We must talk about this. Winning is important to me, too, and—"

"Champions aren't late."

"It does not matter. This a charity event, not a competition. And your dance card is empty, no?"

Ouch! Still, she lifted her chin, despite his low blow. "Not the point. People are still watching."

"Not everything is work, Shan. Must you be so driven? Enjoy life a little."

"I enjoy winning." Her teeth hurt from grinding them together.

"Except for dance, you have no life. When did you last go on a date?"

"Are you keeping track?"

"I grow tired of your so-serious attitude. Maybe you need to go to *Sneak Peek* and um, how do you say, let loose like me."

"We have the biggest competition of our careers in eight days, and you think I need to get laid?"

"Yes."

Shanna tried not to see red—along with violet, crimson, and magenta.

Kristoff met her angry gaze squarely. "Until you smile and be nice, you are not fun to dance with. You will certainly make no money for the cause tonight in this mood."

It might be uncharitable of her, but it was hard to think about someone else's cause when her own was falling apart. And the fact that he took no responsibility for putting her in this mood really annoyed her.

"Go to hell, Mr. Palavin!" She made to stalk past him.

He grabbed her arm. "You are angry. I fucked up, yes. I am sorry. I know what this means to you. But no matter how much I apologize, no matter that we have become friends in the past year, will you forgive me? Stand by me? By tomorrow, I believe you will be holding auditions because everyone knows any partner who is a liability to your ambition is quickly replaced." He grabbed the flash drive off the table. "There is a reason your dance card is empty tonight and everyone calls you the Bitch of the Ballroom. In the past, I have defended you, but now... Have a lovely time alone."

~

"*A*re you staring at that *ramera* again?"

Alejandro Diaz ripped his gaze away from Shanna York and sent a rebuking stare to his dance partner. "*Mamá,* you've been listening to gossip. We do not know her well enough to know if she's a bitch."

But he'd looked at her enough to know he wanted her bad. Her soft blond hair shone under the lights like a halo around her face. Those blue, blue eyes projected a little-girl-lost quality that made him want to hold her close and whisper reassurances. But the fiery way she moved her killer body when she danced, like she performed sex to music, made him hard as hell.

Oh, he had fantasies about her—about taking her to *Sneak Peek* and melting away all that icy reserve by stripping her down, tying her up, filling her full of his cock...while she wondered if they were being watched. Would she get off knowing that others could see the rise of her pleasure and hear the gasps of her orgasms as he gave them to her, one after the other? The way Shanna danced lured men in, as if she loved having their eyes on her, as if she craved hot stares and knowing they had even hotter fantasies with her at the center.

How would she feel if she knew *he* harbored lots of fantasies about her?

His mother shook her head. "Hmm. You met her once. She was not polite."

Not true. She'd been very polite, in an icy, reserved way. In retrospect, he'd come on too strong, been too direct. Clearly not the way to approach an independent woman who valued being in control.

"Tonight is another night." He turned his mother around the dance floor in a gentle waltz. And he watched Shanna.

Her appearance lived up to her ice princess reputation in a short, silvery, barely-there costume of sequins and crystals. She was unsmiling and a bit aloof. He'd love to melt her.

"There are other single women here. Girls who are good. And Catholic. And yet you focus on the *ramera rubia*."

"*Mamá*," Alejandro warned. "You don't know her personally. Just because she's blond does not mean she's a bitch."

He sighed. He loved his mother and owed her much. As a single woman, she'd raised him with loving arms and a firm hand, since his father had left them just before Alejandro became a teenager. She hadn't given him much in the way of luxuries as a kid, but she'd made up for it by providing all the affection and guidance he'd needed. As an adult, however, he realized she was incredibly old-fashioned.

"Spending too much time at that club of yours has confused your thinking, *mijo*. Nothing but *putas* there."

Ali laughed. His mother didn't disapprove of the club...but she only knew about the bar and pool tables, the dart boards and the dance floor. She had no idea what went on upstairs.... Better to keep it that way.

He made damn good money as *Sneak Peek's* co-owner. Between that, his savings, and his other investments, he'd been able to buy his mother a condo and a new car, set up a trust for her, and give her a bit of luxury in the last two years. She just wanted him to settle down, marry, have babies. *Mamá* had made that *very* clear.

He would...in his own good time.

"Let's not argue." He twirled her toward the punch table, not far from where Shanna sat alone. As he looked at the gorgeous dancer again, he had to fight the rise of his erection. *Not here, not now...but soon.*

His mother followed the line of his sight. "*Dios mío*, can you not look at one other woman tonight?"

No. He'd come tonight specifically to cozy up to Shanna York. What a happy coincidence that making his mother's night would help him to make his own.

"*Mamá*, did you sign up to dance with your favorites tonight?"

She shook her head. "No."

"Why not?"

"Alejandro, it is too much money. You paid for me to be here, and that is enough. I will watch."

And send a disapproving stare every time he rumbaed Shanna into a dark corner? Not truly enjoy herself? No.

"You will dance."

He stopped her before the punch table and handed her a drink. While she sipped, he eased over to the table that held the dancers' cards. There were still a few empty slots available to foxtrot or tango with some of her favorites. And Shanna's card was completely empty. He wrote his mother's name onto the empty spaces of the male dancers' cards, then he wrote his own on Shanna's in every space. With a smile, he called the attendant over.

After settling dances for his mother, he handed the volunteer, a perky brunette, Shanna's card. "I would like to purchase all these dances, as well."

The brunette looked at it and frowned. "Hers? All of them?"

"*Sí.*"

"That's three thousand dollars." She pointed out with a hint of incredulity.

He handed her his credit card. "Then I will have the pleasure of knowing more children will have full bellies and be attending school, while I dance with a beautiful woman."

The woman sent him a look that plainly said she thought he was unhinged. "She isn't known for keeping her partners long. You may not last the whole night."

For what he had in mind, a night was all he needed.

With a smile, he finished paying, then found his mother.

"The charity dances start in five minutes, and you will be busy." He handed her a schedule of her partners.

"Alejandro! You spend too much money on an old woman. I cannot dance so much."

"*Mamá*, you are barely fifty. It's only money, and I can afford it. Enjoy yourself."

He certainly planned to.

2

he event's emcee announced the beginning of the charity dances, and Shanna poised herself in a chair, plastic smile in place, at the edge of the ballroom floor.

People around her were beginning to pair up for the first of the dances, names and smiles being exchanged. She tossed her hair off her shoulders. That twisting of her stomach was not a pang of hurt. She didn't care if no one bid on her dances. Sitting back would give her an opportunity to observe her competition, since most of the other dancers were here...just in case she and Kristoff still had a chance to win, in spite of his indiscreet sex life.

Tomorrow, she'd get to the bottom of that shocking video. She wasn't giving up on years of hard work and her dreams of being a champion without a fight.

"I believe this dance is mine."

Shanna followed the deep voice and looked up into an incredibly handsome face. Strong features, burning hazel eyes, heavy five-o'clock shadow, perfectly tailored gray suit with a vavoom red tie. Her heart lurched; this one had sin written all over him.

He also looked familiar. She stared, hesitating, but the more she thought about it, the more certain she became. Somewhere, somehow, they'd crossed paths before.

"Have we met?"

He smiled, all dazzling charm, oozing Latin charisma and hot sex. "Yes. Three months ago. The Bartolino Foundation thing."

That night rushed back to her with overwhelming clarity. This sexy man with his killer smile, flirting outrageously and whispering shocking, hot suggestions as he tangoed her around the dance floor. At the end of the night, he'd asked her out...while trying to kiss her. She'd refused every would-be swain for the past two years without a single regret. But he sorely tempted her. The man might as well have the word *Distraction* tattooed on his forehead. Dating him was impossible. That night, she'd refused him and disappeared into the crowd. She assumed she'd seen the last of him.

Now she suspected she'd underestimated his resolve.

"Ah, I think you recall that night." A smile lifted the edges of his lips.

"Alejandro, isn't it?"

"Alejandro Diaz, yes."

Shanna drew in a deep breath. Just like their first meeting, he caused an unwelcome dizzying effect, complete with revving heartbeat. *Warning!* When she had to bring a date to a social occasion—the only time she went out—she chose safe men who were too busy with their own work to be demanding and too dull to keep her interest for more than an evening. She just didn't have time for a relationship when she had a dance career that needed all her attention.

This one might as well shout that he'd be both fascinating and determined. He meant to get his way—and have his way with her.

Not if she could help it.

Steeling herself against the impact of his touch, Shanna put her hand in his. No matter how prepared she thought she'd been for the skin-on-skin contact, she'd been wrong. A wild gong of want beat through her the second her palm brushed his. She braced for the rush of heat as she stood.

"The music is starting. Shall we?" He gestured to the dance floor, then eased her forward with a hand at the small of her back.

"Sure." What else could she say? This was his three minutes; he'd paid for them, so she owed him that. But no more.

God, not a second more.

A soft Latin rhythm began to wash the room from the overhead speakers. Sensual, hypnotic, the music spoke of a humid summer night shared by lovers. Shanna nearly groaned. Great, a rumba, the dance of love. The one that most emulated passion and sex. Why now?

On a strong beat, Alejandro grabbed her wrist and pulled her against him. Shanna tried to stop herself from crashing into him by planting a hand on his chest. But her fingers only encountered hard muscle. He was like a rock under that shirt, and given his mile-wide shoulders, she was suddenly sure that seeing him naked would be ten times better than a slice of her favorite sinful chocolate cake.

He hooked a finger under her chin. Reluctantly, she lifted her gaze to his. The heat in those hazel eyes could melt steel. *Look away. Get away!* But she couldn't. Once her gaze connected with his, she was locked in, fused to him in a way she didn't understand.

That stare sizzled all through her...and settled right between her legs. She felt unable to break his gaze.

Sex had always been something she could take or leave. At the moment, she wanted to take anything he was willing to dish out.

How could he do that to her with just a glance?

As she drew in a deep breath and tried to find her wits, he curled a thick arm around her waist, drawing her even closer. His whole body was hard...every inch of it. From the feel of him, many inches. Shanna trembled to realize he was every bit as interested as she was. Thank god these dances were short.

Then he held out his left hand, palm up. Slowly, she placed her hand in his.

They began to dance. He was incredibly smooth, never dancing on his heels, never losing the beat of the music. Wow, could he move his hips. Perfect figure eights with them. No doubt, he'd learned how to dance very well somewhere along the way.

Basic boxes quickly gave way to an open position, then a cross, which he used as an opportunity to brush his body against hers and caress her hip. An underarm turn led her right back to a basic.

He was good for an amateur. She had an inkling that he might be good at other things, too.

"So, what brings you here tonight?" she asked, grasping at conversational straws. Maybe if she was talking, she wouldn't be thinking about how much this guy turned her on.

"Helping orphans is not a worthwhile cause?"

"It is. Most men would rather simply write a check than ballroom dance."

"I brought my mother. She enjoys these things, and it is a very small thing to do in order to see her smile."

Sexy, a good dancer, family-oriented, crazy handsome—Alejandro seemed like every woman's fantasy and way too good to be true. He must have some terrible flaw she just couldn't see at the moment. If not...she was in a heap of trouble.

Her body temperature was rising with every suggestive look, every sweep of his hand over her waist and low dive on her hip, each brush of his palm that inched toward her ass.

Damn! Why hadn't she found some man to scratch her itch in the last two years? Or even invested in a good vibrator? Maybe if she had, she wouldn't feel wound so tightly right now, so ready to jump on Alejandro and every protruding part of his body.

"That's nice of you," she managed to say.

"Not really. I knew you would be here."

"M-me?"

"Hmm." He led her into another open position, then curled her against his body, hips crushed against hips. She felt way more than his pelvis.

"Certainly you can feel my...enthusiasm to see you again." He laughed, seemingly at himself.

Yeah. His enthusiasm was sizeable and very hard to miss.

Then he leaned her back over his arm in an exaggerated dip and followed her down. Until his face was an inch from her breasts.

Shanna felt him exhale, his warm breath caressed her cleavage. Her nipples beaded instantly.

Slowly, he lifted her upright again, then spun her around until her back rested against his chest. He nestled his erection in the small of her back. The flat of his palm covered her abdomen, and he took her other hand in his. The gesture probably looked possessive. It certainly felt that way.

Straight ahead, she saw Kristoff dancing with a thin, middle-aged woman with hair a dubious shade of red. He peered at her with a questioning brow raised.

Alejandro led her to swivel her hips against his, in time with the music. Kristoff didn't miss a second of it. In fact, as Shanna looked around, she realized they'd gathered quite a bit of attention.

A blast of moisture flooded her sex.

"Everyone is watching," he whispered.

"I see that." Her voice shook.

He bent and lifted her leg, wrapping her calf around his thigh and urging her head to fall back to his shoulder. Their eyes met, their mouths inches apart.

Shanna felt stripped down, as if she was naked under Alejandro's knowing gaze. God, if he didn't stop that, she'd melt against him right here, right now.

"Men are watching you, wanting you."

He grabbed her thigh, spun her around to face him, then placed that thigh over his hip. They rested nearly hip to hip again. As he leaned back slightly, he forced her chest against his. Still, she couldn't break his stare.

"And you like it," he whispered.

She opened her mouth to deny it, but Alejandro's gaze stopped her, warning her before she could do anything foolish, like lie.

"I can tell you do."

The intensity of his stare, the way in which he'd dug past her icy defenses, seemed to see the real her, and guessed her dirty secret... He was a walking wet dream. He was her worst nightmare.

How had he known she loved being watched?

Alejandro swayed with the music in the opposite direction, bringing her body with him. With a gentle caress of her cheek, he directed her gaze back to his—all while making it look like a part of the dance.

"You know you do," he murmured. "You love that most every man in the room would kill to have your body against his and an up-close view of that smoldering sensuality melting the ice you wrap yourself in."

His words made her shake because they were so true. "Stop."

He performed an open step, then brought her back for a box. "Their stares cling to you as you lure them in with the sway of your hips to the beat of the music. They are drawn to your femininity. Their gazes caress your breasts as your chest lifts with every move and breath. They watch the movements of your sleek thighs and wish they could lie between them."

A glance around proved he was totally right. Easily a dozen men were openly watching she and Alejandro dance, their gazes ranging from more than mildly interested to sizzling with heat. Desire vibrated deep inside her, pulsing under her clit. How wet could she get before she stained the front of her thin costume?

And how had Alejandro known exactly what turned her on?

Most people had only seen the driven dancer who yearned to win and find some way to make her family proud. No one else had seen the woman inside who used dance to express the sexuality she otherwise repressed. No one.

This man had known her secret in the blink of an eye. He'd all but mocked her chilly reserve. He looked at her as if he could see beyond her façade, to the fear and emptiness that fed her ambition.

Thankfully, the music ended.

"Thank you for an interesting evening, Mr. Diaz. Perhaps our paths will cross again." But not if she could help it.

Still, he didn't let go. Instead, he continued to stare with that sultry hint of a smile. "The evening is not over. I bought all of your dances tonight. Every last one."

Shanna stared at him, wide eyed and stunned. Panicked. That was bad. Very bad. Just being in his arms and hearing his words made her feel vulnerable in a way she didn't like and would not tolerate.

And she was stuck with him for the next three hours? Lord, she was in so much trouble.

"Why?"

"I enjoy watching you being watched and the way it arouses you. I love knowing that so many men in the room are fantasizing about slaking their lust with you—"

"You don't know what other men are thinking," she protested.

"Yes, I do. It is exactly what I'm thinking. It is even more delicious because I alone am holding you in my arms."

Oh, god. "This conversation is inappropriate."

"Honesty disturbs you?"

"I'm not...I—I don't get aroused by knowing that men are watching me."

"Really?"

He urged her into a cross again. No sooner than she turned to step into the next box, he pushed against her hand, sending her spinning to face the wall. Then he was behind her, cradling her swaying hips, his mouth hovering just over her sensitive nape in a darkened corner of the ballroom.

Shanna shivered as he exhaled on her sensitive flesh and gripped her hips.

Then he reached around to place his hand flat on her stomach again...but he aimed high, flattening his palm on the upper swells of her chest and smoothing his way down.

"Hard nipples," he commented. "Such pretty, edible, want-to-suck-them-in-my-mouth buds."

She opened her mouth to stop him with a hiss, but he kept tantalizing her as he caressed his way south, down her ribs, over her stomach, until his fingers brushed the front of her costume right over her very wet sex. He lingered. Shame and arousal crashed inside her. She closed her eyes.

"You're always wet when you dance in public...like now, aren't you?"

At his touch, his words, pleasure spiked, hitting her full force, like a blast from a raging fire. She sucked in a breath. Damn it, why did he have to be right?

If he could read her that well after a few minutes with her, Shanna knew he'd quickly dig deeper into her soul unless she put distance between them now.

"Stop," she demanded in her best ice-queen voice.

"Answer me, *querida*."

"No."

He danced her to face him again as one song segued into the next, this one a waltz.

"Do not be embarrassed. Your arousal turns me on. It's one of the reasons I chose not to give up when you rebuffed me at the Bartolino event. I want that arousal," he whispered in her ear. "I want it in my hands, my mouth, all around my cock when I fuck you. Will you wonder then exactly who is watching us?"

His words hit her like lava, sizzling her skin, charring her resistance and sanity. No one had ever talked to her like that. Between her brothers and the bitchiness she wore like armor, no one had dared.

God, even without uttering a word, Alejandro was stunning. When he murmured that sort of sin, he didn't just turn her on; he turned her inside out.

He was dangerous. She could see getting lost in such a man and his smoldering promise of spectacular sex—the kind she'd never experienced.

"That's enough," she forced herself to say.

"We haven't started. I think about undressing you under soft lights, your back to my front and letting my hand smooth your dress from your lush curves. I ache to brush my palms over your hard nipples before I roll them between my fingers. I fantasize about feeling my way lower, down to that soft, wet pussy, then grazing your hard clit. And stroking you until you come. I obsess about bending you over and filling you with my cock—all while you suspect the hot stares of strangers rake you. Want you."

Desire pulsed, flared with every mental image he created. She could *see* herself naked, flushed, writhing under his hands or as he impaled her. She could feel herself dissolving at the thought of orgasming for him—and a roomful of aroused men.

This was dangerous. Bad. Wrong. *No, no, no.*

"I said that's enough!" Her voice shook as hard as the rest of her.

He kept on, as if she'd never uttered a protest. "I am part owner of a club where you could express yourself in any way you like. In every way that gets you off. *Sneak Peek* was made for women like you."

Sneak Peek? The club where Kristoff's video had been filmed in his soon-to-be-infamous threesome? That jolted her.

"I know what goes on there."

A smiled toyed with those sensual lips of his. "Good. If we weren't waltzing now, I would reach between those sleek thighs of yours, and I bet I would find out you're even wetter now than the last time I touched you."

Shanna wanted to lie, but she didn't trust him not to waltz her in a corner and test his theory.

"I need to use the ladies' room."

He hesitated, then released her. "By all means."

She turned away, resisting the urge to run to the sanctuary of her dressing room. No, she would walk. Calmly. *Breathe in, breathe out.*

And screw charity. Yes, Alejandro had paid his money. He'd gotten his dance and his cheap feel, too. He could pat himself on the back, knowing that he'd dug up her naughty secret and rubbed it in her face. She wasn't coming back. If she ever saw him at one of these charity events again, she'd run in the other direction. Fast.

Before she could take the first step, he grabbed her wrist and whirled her around. Suddenly off balance, she collided against his chest. Her head snapped back...her mouth right under his.

"Come to *Sneak Peek*. There, I will fulfill your every fantasy."

Of that, she had no doubt. But no way could she give him that chance.

3

"So I've got two choices, both really lousy." Shanna sighed as she stirred her hot tea at the outdoor café's wrought iron table the next morning. "Either I stick it out and hope this threat is just a sick joke or I dump Kristoff, try to find yet another new partner, and wait a season or two before we mesh well enough to win anything."

Jonathan winced. "Don't you think it's time you stop dropping partners, love? Your reputation in that area isn't exactly sparkling."

She regarded her former dance partner with a frosty stare. "Ending our partnership was a mutual decision."

The handsome Aussie reached for her hand across the table. "The handwriting was on the wall. We weren't going to make it. I didn't want to win as badly as you did. And sleeping together was a terrible mistake."

Shanna wanted to deny his assertion, but couldn't. Jonathan simply hadn't possessed her drive to win. They'd both known it. Their one night of impulsive sex had merely brought their problems to the fore.

Admittedly, sex between them had been stupid. But a late-night practice, Jonathan suffering a recent break-up with his fiancée,

Shanna fearing their days of competing together were numbered, hours upon hours of nothing but sexually-charged dances, with the tension between them so thick... The dam holding their restraint had burst.

Afterward, their partnership had gone from strained to doomed. Her ambition on the dance floor hadn't meshed well with his need to check out to deal with his recent turmoil. Belatedly, Shanna had realized he needed more emotional support from a partner than she'd given. Their fights had become hellacious. They'd said terrible things, and he'd walked out.

In retrospect, the end of their dance partnership had been best for both of them. Jonathan's fiancée had returned, and he'd retired to married life and modeling. After a few months of silence between them, he'd reached out to her. Over the last eighteen months, they'd repaired their friendship. During that time, Shanna had been happily paired with Kristoff...until she'd seen his porn-inspired deeds.

"Let's not rehash ancient history," Jonathan said. "You came to me with a problem. Are you sleeping with Kristoff?"

Shanna shook her head. "Of course not. Until I saw the video, I thought he was firmly in the gay column."

"At least that's one less complication."

The early-morning breeze whipped through her hair. Shanna looked down into her steaming mug. "I have to decide what to do. I don't want to lose Kristoff as a partner. Training a new one would take so much time. But if the judges get their hands on that footage..."

"That would be devastating. The old crones would crucify you. The men...they'd either try to bury or debauch you."

"Exactly. I want to strangle Kristoff every time the realization that he's jeopardized everything hits me."

"In the dance department, you're well-matched. Kristoff is a fabulous athlete who wants to win every bit as badly as you. Admit that much."

She rolled her eyes. "I suppose."

"Stop," he demanded. "I know you too well. Everyone else may buy that puffed-up bitch act, but we both know better. It took me years to realize you're not half as pissed as you are afraid. You're trembling at the thought of being vulnerable and of not holding that trophy so you can finally prove to your family that you're a champion. Is Daddy's opinion really more important than friendship? It's okay to stand by your friends, even if your family will disapprove."

God, he had her number.

"Have you taken up psychotherapy on the side, Freud?"

"Just calling your bluff."

"I came to you for help, and you're giving me hell." She stood and grabbed her paper mug.

"Sorry," Jonathan murmured, looking like he wanted to say more on the subject. Mercifully, he didn't. "Do you have any other information about the video or its delivery that might help you track down the blackmailer? Or did Kristoff know anything about how it was made?"

"No, I don't think Kristoff has a clue. But last night, the owner of the sex club in which the footage was filmed tried to seduce me out of my panties. If the event hadn't been for charity—"

"You know where this tape was made?"

She nodded. "A place called *Sneak Peek*."

"The club for voyeurs and exhibitionists?"

Jonathan knew about that place? "Yes."

He sat back in his chair, a taunting smile curling up his mouth. Shanna felt her heart seize. He looked at her as if he knew being watched made her wet. Did he? Did every man who watched her dance?

Thankfully, he didn't go there. "So when you danced with this mate, did you talk to him, see what he knows about the video and its creation?"

"No." She'd been too busy resisting his seduction, trying to fend off his unnerving ability to see past her defenses.

"There you go." He shrugged. "Maybe he can help you track down who's blackmailing Kristoff."

Shanna gripped her tea. Jonathan was right. The answer had

been staring her in the face. Alejandro could find out exactly who had filmed Kristoff.

All she had to do was put herself in his path again and pray she could resist him.

❧

"*I* need your help."

Alejandro Diaz looked up at the female with the trembling voice hovering in the door of his office. Platinum hair pulled tightly away from her unusually pale face. Blue eyes smudged with the bruises of sleeplessness. Shanna York. Here, in his office.

Well, didn't this make his morning interesting?

"Long trip to the ladies' room," he drawled.

She lifted her chin—her silent way of telling him she would not bend her pride to apologize for having deserted him last night. Alejandro frowned...though he was silently amused.

"You came on too strong. Again. I needed to put space between us."

"And now you do not? Today, I'm supposed to forget that I enjoyed a dance and a half, rather than the eight I paid for."

"You gave that money to charity."

"To be with you. The charity was the cherry on top."

"You paid for the opportunity to dance with me, not seduce me."

Why not both? he wanted to ask, but tactically retreated from that line of questioning. Starting a fight with Shanna wasn't the way to entice her to stay. Raising her hackles would not get him the up close and very personal time he wanted with her.

"Perhaps I succeeded, since you have come to *Sneak Peek* because... What was that you said? Ah, yes. You need me."

"I'd still be avoiding you if I didn't need your help," she shot back. "Which I happen to need now. Please."

Hmm. She'd likely choked on that word. Shanna was stubborn and tough and wore her ice like armor. No doubt it warded off most men.

He was made of stronger stuff.

Alejandro stood and faced her. "What can I do for you? Take you on a tour? We have great facilities."

Her expression softened. "It's a beautiful place. I was expecting something..."

"Dark? Sleazy? Dirty?"

She hesitated. "Glass-and-chrome seedy, yes. This is really...warm."

That's what had attracted him to the house in the beginning. Ali thanked God every time he set foot in the place that his business partner, Del, had agreed with his choice of locations. Its shimmering white plaster walls glowed Hollywood golden when the sun set over the hills of Los Angeles. The expansive gardens had a charming Spanish Revival feel, complete with decorative tile that rimmed the pool and outlined the patio steps leading to the second floor. The bars, both indoors and outdoors, welcomed guests. Converting the house into a club had given it the feel of an intimate party, rather than a bunch of strangers getting naked together. That instant comfort level was one of the reasons he and Del had been so successful since opening *Sneak Peek*. That and good business sense.

Alejandro shrugged. "I took one look at the house and fell in love. Cary Grant built it in the 1920's. The previous owners started restoring it about ten years ago...and ran out of money. Del and I spent a small fortune to buy the place and finish renovating. I have not regretted it."

"It's gorgeous."

"As are you. Since it's clear you are not here for me to seduce, what can I do for you?"

Her charmed smile disappeared. The tense hand-clasping returned. "My dance partner and I have a...situation. A delicate one. Kristoff has been here, as a customer, right?"

"I'm not at liberty to answer that. Privacy is something we protect fiercely here at *Sneak Peek*. I hope you understand."

"But that's just it. Someone invaded his privacy. They filmed him..." She shook her head. "It would be better if I showed you."

Alejandro frowned as Shanna reached into an oversized bag hanging from her shoulder and extracted a flash drive in a clear plastic case. She handed it to him, her expression tense. He popped it into his laptop.

Two and a half minutes later, anger boiled his blood.

"Where did you get this?"

"Someone left it in my dressing room last night just before the benefit began, along with a note telling me that if we competed in the upcoming California Dance Star, this footage will be sent to all the judges."

"And neither you nor Kristoff have any idea who sent it?"

She shook her head. "That's why I'm here. I was hoping you could help me. That competition means...everything to me. I've worked *years* to win this."

As driven as she was, as ambitious as rumor painted her, Ali believed it. She had dumped three partners in the last five years. One after breaking his leg badly skiing just before dance season began. The next partner had been history when he dropped her during a lift —in the middle of a competition. The third...he was a mystery. There one day, gone the next. Alejandro's mother had the pulse on all her favorite and not-so-favorite dancers. *Mamá* said there had been rumors of a torrid—but brief—affair between she and Jonathan Smythe.

Alejandro extracted the flash drive, slotted it back in its case, and handed it to her. "There are absolutely no still or video cameras allowed in the club. Period. That is part of our strict privacy policy."

"Which someone clearly violated."

"Yes, because that isn't security footage. If it was, it would be black and white and from an aerial view. It certainly wouldn't be in full color and focused in tight on the action." Alejandro rose, paced.

This was very bad news. People paid a lot of money to enjoy themselves at the club anonymously. Often high profile people. Stars, senators, diplomats. If that privacy was compromised and people found out... He didn't want to think about what it might do to their business.

"Would you excuse me for a moment?" he asked.

"Yes."

Alejandro pulled his cell phone from his pocket and hit the speed dial button to reach his partner.

"Del?" he asked after hearing a familiar voice rumble at the other end. "We have a situation you ought to know about."

"I'll be there in five."

It was more like ten minutes later when Del sauntered in, buttoning his shirt and wearing a smile. His mussed hair explained why. Damn, it was barely past ten in the morning, but his buddy had already been getting busy. A glance at Shanna reminded him that he hadn't been busy like that in longer than he cared to admit...and he knew exactly who he would like to change that fact with.

"What's up?"

"Del, this is Shanna York. She is a professional ballroom dancer. Shanna, my business partner, Del."

Shanna held out a prim little hand for a professional shake. Del, being the Frenchman he was, enveloped her hand and brought it to his mouth for a soft kiss. "*Enchanté.*"

No doubt he was enchanted, but this wasn't a free-for-all.

"Back off," Alejandro growled in Del's ear.

His friend sent him a dark-eyed glance full of curiosity. Ali wasn't saying a word. Del wasn't stupid. He understood.

When Shanna snatched her hand away, Ali had to repress a gratified smile. When had any woman ever pulled away from Del? Never. Usually, they threw themselves at his dark stubble, wealth, and bad attitude.

"This is Shanna's situation..."

Ali clued Del in, and Shanna provided the flash drive for viewing again. After the clip ended, Del was gnashing his teeth and looking none too happy.

"I wish I knew who to beat the shit out of for violating the rules."

"Me, too," Alejandro agreed.

"Okay, so you don't know off the top of your heads who might have done it," Shanna said. "I'm assuming you know in which room this...event took place?"

"Yes," the men answered together.

"Maybe by figuring out who might have used the room in the last week, you can get a list of likely suspects. Do you keep records?"

"For payment purposes, yes," Del confirmed. "But that room, it's likely been used at least fifty times since that recording was made."

Shanna did the math. "Ten...events in there a *day*?"

With a shrug, Alejandro smiled. "We go through a lot of sheets."

Del laughed, the sound hearty and male.

"Aren't you two cute? Freshman Frat Boy and his sidekick, Horny." She rolled her eyes. "I'm assuming you don't want it known that someone is sneaking into your club and recording your guests' most private actions without their consent or knowledge."

He and Del sobered up quickly. She was right. Business now. Pleasure...soon.

Still, his mind took a little detour. Her shock about the room's constant use was amusing, and it pleased him that she did not understand how addicting watching—and being watched—could be. Yet. He intended to introduce her to that delight.

"Of course we don't want our guests compromised," Del cut in smoothly. "We could make a list of all the guests who have used this room in the last week, but I doubt it would help. In all honesty, I would never have believed any of our members would violate such a cardinal rule. The fee to join is steep enough to attract only the most serious. Our rules are absolute; there is no room for gray. We also have ways of ensuring that anyone who violates our rules finds themselves unwelcome at similar clubs elsewhere."

"This feels to me as if you were targeted specifically," Alejandro said. "The note was delivered to your dressing room, so close to a major competition..."

"That's it! Do any of my competitors belong to your club?"

Ali looked at Del, who looked back at him. That was the great thing about having been friends for nearly a decade. They could almost read each other's minds. Answering the question wasn't really giving away information...

"No. Kristoff is the only ballroom dancer and he's recent. He came highly recommended and has been very active since he joined."

"I'll bet." She snorted. "And here I thought he was your average, garden-variety gay man..."

Del choked. Alejandro resisted the urge to laugh himself.

Shanna swatted his shoulder. "Okay, clearly that's untrue. You two can stop snickering now."

Alejandro couldn't resist her ruffled feathers for another second. He was dying to soothe them...right before he melted her.

"What about any of my former dance partners?" She directed the question to Alejandro. Not that she suspected Jonathan, but the first two hated her. "Do you know who they are?"

"No and yes. None of your former partners are members."

"Hmm." Shanna bit a pink, bee-stung lip as she thought. "Have any of your other members indicated this breach of privacy has been a problem for them?"

"Hell no! Whoever took the footage isn't one of your competitors, but it is someone who knows about your world of ballroom. About you and what you value."

"Yes," Del agreed. "Someone who knew that competition was coming up and that the judges would punish you if such footage became public."

"Any ideas who among your members that could be?" Shanna prompted.

Again, Ali looked at Del, who shook his head. "Not a clue. I could ask you the same question. Who are your enemies?"

Shanna's blue eyes darted around as if scanning her memories. "No one else I can think of. If it's not a former partner or a competitor, I know of no one who hates me enough to want to destroy me."

"Well, if any guest was a friend of one of your former partners or competitors, we have no way of knowing."

"True..." Shanna nibbled nervously on a hangnail, then, as if realizing she'd done something less than perfect, she stopped. "What about your employees? Do any of them have access to video cameras and those rooms?"

Del shook his head. "We have four types of employees: security, housekeeping, waitstaff, and bar crew. That's it. They are paid to be invisible unless they're needed. None of those employees should be anywhere near a room when it's in use. All the watching and exhibiting is done for and with fellow members."

"So, another dead end..."

"It appears," Del agreed, then looked his way. His buddy had the glint of the devil in his eyes. "That we should draw this blackmailer out."

"Have Kristoff come back and do it again and hope someone makes another recording?" She sounded confused.

"No," Ali said, catching on to the idea. "Kristoff has been recorded. He has served his purpose. It is interesting that whomever recorded him chose to give the video not to him, but to *you*."

"Exactly," Del chimed in. "The blackmailer is trying to get to you. He or she wants *you* to suffer. Kristoff is just one avenue."

"So what are you suggesting I do?"

One more time, Alejandro and Del exchanged a meaningful glance.

"I think, *querida*, he's suggesting that I arrange a scene for you here and see if we can catch him red-handed in the act of filming you."

Shanna's jaw dropped. "Are you insane!! You think I should come here and get naked and..."

"Spend a little time showing our members what you enjoy," Alejandro supplied.

"I can't give this creep any more ammunition to ruin me."

"He already has everything he needs to discredit you with the judges. But I do not think he's actually trying to prevent you from competing, as much as he's attacking you. This feels personal, not business related. If you want to find out who is behind this, you must...expose yourself."

"I'm not into that!"

After last night, Alejandro knew better, but now wasn't the time to remind her. "Pretend, if you must. But I believe the plan will work."

Shanna hesitated, as if she was pondering his words. "*If* I agree to this crazy scheme, can I do...whatever it is alone?"

Alejandro couldn't resist the grin spreading across his face. "Plenty of our members would jump through rings of fire to see you touch yourself."

"Wait. You mean masturbate for an audience?" She turned terribly white under her usual golden glow.

"Even the thought of it makes me hard," he whispered for her ears alone.

"Absolutely not!"

"No? Then I will be more than happy to assist you," Alejandro volunteered.

"I'll bet."

"It would be more believable...and more blackmail-worthy," Del chimed in. "I will hide in the room and watch all doors, windows, and passersby—see if I can identify our camera-wielding asshole."

Her jaw dropped. "It's bad enough to contemplate getting naked with the Latin Lover, here. But having you watch? No."

That horror on her face was nothing but a lie. Her suddenly hard nipples told him that. She was scared—of herself, of him, of whatever was fueling her ambition. Suddenly, he wanted to get to the bottom of it all. He wanted to learn her.

"What troubles you? Is the idea too arousing?"

Shanna sent Ali a hard glare. "It's too weird. And it won't work."

"What are your better ideas?"

Pausing, Shanna bit her lip. Oh, yes, she was thinking her options through.

A few moments later, she gritted her teeth. "I don't have a better idea. But there's got to be one."

"This guy will return to the scene of the crime if we dangle the right bait in front of him. Catching him in the act of creating or delivering a video is the only way to be certain he's the guilty party."

Shanna's firm ass outlined in white capri pants that made Ali's tongue melt as she paced the floor and contemplated in a silence broken only by her high-heels.

"God, I can't believe I'm actually considering this. I must be out of my mind."

"It may be the only way to figure out who's trying to screw up your career," Del supplied.

"Which is the only reason I haven't already said no."

"Would you feel more comfortable if I showed you the room and all the places Del can hide in order to catch this bastard?"

Del sent him a knowing smile.

She nodded. "I'm not sure this will work, but maybe if I see the room, something will occur to me."

"You two come up with the plan and let me know. I need to get back to my...company." Del clapped him on the back, kissed Shanna's hand again, and disappeared upstairs.

In charged silence, Alejandro led Shanna down a hall and up another set of stairs, to the play rooms. At the second door on the left, he paused and eased it open into a dark, enclosed space.

Beyond the handful of comfortable chairs and a long, cushy sofa lay the far corner of the room, which comprised the stage, currently devoid of guests. The muted lights in that corner shined down on a sleek bed with four chrome posts and matching restraints.

"Oh." Her voice fluttered beside him.

Alejandro would bet this week's take that Shanna was envisioning herself on that stage, her pussy shoved full of his cock—and a rapt audience watching. He'd bet next week's take that she was uncomfortably aroused.

"Other members sit here or look through the windows at the far end of the room and watch the scene. From the clip you showed me, I suspect your blackmailer sat in the room, here." Alejandro pointed to a small chair in the shadows, a mere three feet from the end of the bed. "He either used a zoom lens or moved the chair closer to the bed to get the tight penetration shots. But we won't know for sure until we catch him."

"I understand." Her voice trembled even more.

Alejandro smiled to himself as he turned and pointed to a bare wall. "Through here is a doorway, accessible only from the security area. See, no knob on this side. We can position the cameras to watch this chair. Del can either monitor the room from the bank of cameras or from the chairs in the far corner."

"I see." She cleared her throat. "If you have security cameras viewing this room, can't you review the footage and see if anyone holding a video camera is in the shot?"

He shook his head. "They point only at the stage areas. Our primary concern here is for the safety of the players. We make sure everything that happens on stage is consensual. If there's a hint that something is not, we bust in. But we do not regularly monitor the audience. For this scene only, we will change the camera positioning."

"Wouldn't the blackmailer be able to spot Del if he was watching from one of those chairs?" She gestured across the room.

"Come with me." Alejandro held out his hand to her.

Shanna looked at it, then looked at him, before reluctantly placing her hand in his. Immediately, sparks danced in his palm, down his fingers. God, he could hardly wait to get his hands on this woman.

For the moment, he led her across the room instead to a dark pair of padded armchairs. He gestured for Shanna to sit in one. He plunked down in the other.

"In this corner, the light is too dim for anyone in the audience to discern more than a shadow. Players cannot see back in this corner. It's a good place for Del to hide, if you want him nearby."

"It's dark."

A click and a whoosh alerted Alejandro to the fact the players' stage door had opened. He glanced at his watch. Noon. Right on time.

In walked a broad man dressed in leather pants, a half mask—and nothing else. Colorful tattoos covered his left arm. In his right hand, he clutched a woman's fingers.

As small as he was big, as delicate as he was strong, the petite redhead followed him to the bed. She wore a flowing, floral skirt that ended at mid-thigh, a button-down blouse in a soft ivory, and a pair of pink high-heeled sandals.

"Are you wearing a bra, slut?" he asked.

"No, Master."

"Show me."

Without pause, she unbuttoned her blouse to reveal a flat stomach, fair skin, and pink nipples that stood straight out and begged for attention.

Shanna gasped. "We shouldn't be watching this."

"They come here knowing that being watched is not only possible, but probable. It turns them on," he whispered. "Shh."

"Good," the Master in leather praised, petting one of her breasts in reward. "Are you wearing panties?"

"No, Master."

"Show me."

The small woman lifted her skirt to reveal slender thighs and a pussy devoid of all hair. Beside Alejandro, Shanna tensed.

"Excellent." The Master cupped her mound and fondled her. "Who do you belong to?"

"You, Master."

"Who decides what's right for your body?"

"You, Master."

"Take off your skirt, lie back, and spread your legs."

The woman complied without hesitation. Even at this distance, once her thighs parted, Alejandro could see a little silver bar passing through the hood of her clit.

"She's...pierced." Shanna sounded shocked.

"Yes," Ali answered. "He marked her. Shh."

"Pretty," said the man in leather as he stared. "Has it healed?"

"Yes, Master."

"Does it arouse you when you walk?"

"Yes, Master."

"Do you rub yourself and make yourself come?"

"No, Master. You did not give me permission."

"That's right. I didn't. You're wet."

"Yes, Master."

"Do you need to be fucked?"

"Yes, Master. Please," the redhead pleaded.

The large man said nothing. He merely walked to all four corners of the bed, restraining his submissive into the built-in cuffs.

"As a reward for your obedience, you will be well fucked." The Master snapped his fingers.

In walked another man, completely naked. Young, blond, somewhat thin—but very well hung.

"This is Micah. He will fuck you now. If you please him and obey me, you may suck my cock as a reward. Do you understand?"

"Yes, Master." Her smile said the idea excited her.

Shanna gripped the arms of her chair and stared at the trio with wide eyes. "She's going to let a complete stranger have sex with her just because he said so?"

"He wants to watch her be fucked, and she has given him domain over her body. She obeys his commands. That is their relationship. Shh."

By now, the blond man had a condom on his thick cock and was easing onto the bed.

"Micah," the man barked. "Test that piercing first. With your tongue."

The younger man smiled. "With pleasure."

"I will tell you when you have permission to come, slut."

"Yes, Master," she panted as Micah took his first swipe across her clit with his tongue and groaned.

The woman lifted her hips to Micah, who used the opportunity to fit his arms under her thighs and grip her, holding her wet folds against his mouth. He licked her unmercifully, insistent lashes with his tongue, and toyed with the little bar piercing the hood of her clit.

Master shucked off his pants, pulled out a wide cock with a pierced head, and stroked slowly as he watched.

Soon, the redhead was flushed and panting, mewling and pleading for release.

"Stop," said the Master.

Micah lifted his head slowly, his lips wet and glossy.

The woman whimpered.

"Are you ready for Micah to fuck you?"

"Yes, Master. Please, yes!"

"Good girl. When I give you permission, you may show me how pretty you are when you come as Micah fucks you."

The woman opened her mouth to answer, but Micah thrust ruthlessly inside her sex first, cutting off all speech. Instead, she gasped, then groaned. Before she recovered, Micah plowed into her again. And again. Once more...

"Come," her master commanded.

She gasped as she orgasmed in a spectacular tensing of limbs and jolting of muscles. Micah gritted his teeth, looking like a man hanging by a thread.

"Beautiful. Micah will continue to fuck you while you suck my cock. You do not come again until I do."

"Yes...Master," she said in a breathy, high gasp just before she turned her head and took Master deep in her mouth.

Beside him, Alejandro noticed Shanna squirming in her seat. Around him, the scent of her arousal wafted. She might pretend to be scandalized, but her body told him exactly how much she loved what was happening before her eyes. How much she liked watching it. He knew from dancing with her that she ached to be watched herself. No doubt in his mind, fucking her in front of a faceless audience would completely arouse Shanna. She couldn't possibly hang onto her ice-bitch persona then.

It didn't take long before Master's buttocks were clenching. He shoved his hand into his slut's red hair and thrust deep in her mouth. Micah had apparently gotten his urge to come under control and now pounded her like a man possessed, beads of sweat dripping down his face, his sides. The woman's skin was a gorgeous shade of aroused rose as she writhed between the two men, giving and receiving pleasure.

Soon, Master tensed, shouted, then erupted into the woman's mouth.

"Come," he told them through clenched teeth.

They did. Loudly, bucking and rocking and clearly enjoying the hell out of themselves.

Moments later, Micah withdrew from the woman's body and disposed of his condom. Master reached out and gave him a brotherly handshake.

"She's one hell of a fuck," Micah commented. "You're lucky, man."

Master nodded and smiled, then Micah disappeared through the door from which he'd emerged. When Master turned his profile to the audience, Ali had no trouble spotting the fact he was hard again. Shanna's gasp told him she'd seen it, too.

Without a word to his woman, Master released her ankles and flipped her onto her belly. As her arms crossed above her head, he urged her to curl her knees under her body, then smacked her ass a half dozen times in harsh, regulated swats. The woman tensed, moaned, bucked.

Then Master reached for the table on the far side of the bed. Moments later, he had lube on his erection and was sliding it inside his woman's rosy ass.

She moaned and writhed when he penetrated her, and he reached around to toy with her clit.

"You're a good girl. Watching you get fucked turns me on, but fucking you myself is heaven. You accept my cock wherever I put it, don't you?"

"Yes! Master, yes!"

Shanna crossed her legs and squirmed again. "Is he…having anal sex with her?"

Alejandro nodded. "It is another show of her submission to him."

She drew in a sharp breath. Even in this light, he could see her hard nipples go even harder. Oh, another something on his long list of things to do to her body once he got the chance. Alejandro managed to keep his smile to himself—barely.

"Seen enough?"

"What?" Shanna tore her eyes away from the couple reluctantly. "O-oh, yes."

He rose and helped her to her feet, then guided her out the door, back into the well-lit hallway. Flushed cheeks, very hard nipples, rapid breaths, pulse beating at her neck. If she owned a vibrator, he'd bet it would get a strenuous workout this afternoon. First time he could ever remember being jealous of plastic and batteries. He'd offer his own flesh, but if he pushed her too hard, too fast, she would run in the other direction.

"So, the scene... How does tomorrow night sound for catching a blackmailer? I will make sure the room is free then."

Shanna took a deep breath. "I haven't made up my mind."

"Whatever you wish. You are the one with a competition in a few days and a blackmailer with an ax to grind."

She sighed in annoyance, clearly not appreciating his reminder that her options were limited. "All right. Tomorrow night."

"Be here by nine." Ali tamped down his smile of triumph with effort. "What sort of scene should I set up? Something for you to do alone?"

Shanna paled a bit more, then mustered her bravado and lifted her chin. "Maybe...you should participate, too. But don't get the wrong idea."

"Wrong idea?"

She sent him a suspicious glare. "I'm serious. This is business. I need to find out who's trying to sabotage me. You need to know who's jeopardizing your club. I'm not interested in you personally."

"Of course not."

"And I'm not sleeping with you."

Who said anything about sleeping? Ali thought.

"Whatever you want, that is what we'll do. Nothing more." *And absolutely nothing less.*

4

"**Y**ou sure about this, man?" Del asked him at eight-thirty the following night as they headed downstairs.

"Yes." Alejandro led the way down the hall, to the second door on the left and pushed it open.

Del closed it behind him. "You want guests in here? They will flip. You're the brains of this place. You almost never play in public. You know the curiosity. There *will* be a crowd."

Ali shrugged. Generally, he watched rather than put on a show, but this was about Shanna tonight, about making her hot. And she adored being watched. He knew that all the way down to the soles of his feet. Now he just needed to let her feel it firsthand and prove it to her.

"Good. I want anyone who attended in the last week, especially if they watched in this room, here tonight. I sent you a list of members who fit that description."

"I got that."

Ali nodded. "Security is looking the names over as well. If Shanna is videoed, we should be able to narrow our list of suspects. I've e-mailed the members who watched last week and hinted at something tantalizing happening in this room tonight. That way, our friend with the video camera is more likely to show up. But wait until nine-fifteen to unlock the door. I want Shanna comfortable. It will be easier for her to let go the first time if the only one watching when we get started is you."

"Even if we only allow the people who've observed in this room recently, others will follow. There will still be a crowd."

Alejandro shrugged. Likely so, but he would deal with it. And with Shanna...

She would be very nervous when she first arrived, but Ali didn't think that would last, especially when she didn't see a gathering crowd right away. And God, he couldn't wait to feel her melt against him, her body opening to accept him deep, her pussy clasping him hard as she came. By then, she'd be desperate for the crowd to see her come undone.

"I need to finish readying the room." Alejandro turned away, eager for the night to begin.

"Wait." When Ali turned back, Del went on, "You're going pretty far to catch this blackmailer."

"The club is important. We both have over a million dollars tied up in it. We cannot afford to allow anyone who would film players without their knowledge to continue as a member here."

"Yeah. Absolutely. It's just...normally you would let security handle it. Or bring in help, if you needed it. This time, you seem to be taking a very personal interest."

"Stop sidestepping your point. What are you saying?"

Del crossed his arms over his wide chest, looking way too pleased. "You like this girl."

"She is very sexy. Why should I not like her?"

Disbelief peppered Del's expression. "There are sexy women here every night more than willing to fuck you. You haven't played with or for the membership in over a year. So there's more to your decision to get on that stage with Shanna than her sexiness."

Mierda. Why couldn't Del leave it alone?

Alejandro sighed. "Yes. I confess, even I am not entirely sure why I am pursuing Shanna so hard. She has rebuffed, left, and insulted me."

"But...?"

Shifting his weight from one foot to the other, Ali sorted through the tangle of his thoughts and feelings. It was damn uncomfortable. He was a gut-instinct sort of guy. If it felt right, he did it. That philosophy had never served him wrong. But even he had to admit that his logic where Shanna was concerned...

There wasn't any.

"Under her brittle façade, she has this lost quality. I don't want to save her, exactly. Or change her. But I cannot resist wanting to hold her. Touch her. And, of course, pleasure her. She looks at me and her expression is like a siren's song. A glance, and I'm hard as hell. A snap from that icy voice I know is hiding a wealth of heat and I'm dying to lay her out, get deep, and melt her into a puddle."

Del laughed. "You're screwed."

"How so?"

"You're falling for this girl."

Was it that obvious?

"And you haven't really touched her yet." Del laughed. "This is going to be fun to watch for more than one reason."

"I'm so happy you're amused. You may fuck off now."

"Ten-four." Del clapped him on the back. "I'll finish making the arrangements with the other employees. The room should be ready. All you need to do is meet Shanna at the door."

No, what he needed to do was please her, not just by lighting her senses and firing her fantasies, but endearing himself to her. Great, but how to do that? Because his gut was telling him that he should not let Shanna out of his life.

~

With a shaking hand, Shanna shoved the door open and entered the cool, air-conditioned space of *Sneak Peek*. At night, the club still had that golden shimmer. But instead of the homey warmth it conveyed during the day, a shimmering glow now illuminated the club. It sparkled and glittered like old Hollywood, except this classic glamour provided the backdrop for today's beautiful people to have dazzling sex.

Del and Alejandro had created a perfect ambiance.

Just past the club's front door, wall-to-wall bodies gyrated to a suggestive techno beat. Couples grinded, intimating sex vertically. In fact, one couple against the wall, shielded by the man's long leather duster, probably *was* having sex. No one seemed to notice or care.

The bar beyond was crowded with people drinking their liquid fortification. Several men crowded around a woman downing shots as if they were waiting for her to give one—or several—of them a sign that she was ready for more personal action.

The whole place oozed sex.

She *so* didn't belong here. Sex had never been her thing. She'd had it, of course. A college boyfriend had been her first, but he hadn't had much experience. Nor had he understood her dancing. They'd spent the relationship fighting because he assumed she was sleeping with her partner at the time, which she hadn't been.

A few years later, she'd had a one-night stand after a wedding. Stupid—and awful. Downright bad sex.

Jonathan...utter disaster—right on the dance floor they'd practiced on for years. She'd clung to him out of desperation. He'd taken her body as if exorcising some demon. The whole episode had lasted less than ten minutes. And created twelve months of pure havoc.

By tonight's end, if she wasn't careful, she would be adding Alejandro to her short list. She'd said she wouldn't have sex with him. But she wondered... Would failing to let loose in a club like this rouse her blackmailer's suspicion? Shanna couldn't let this opportunity slip past her without making the most of it. She had to ferret out this jerk before the California Dance Star.

But that wasn't the only reason she contemplated surrendering to Alejandro. He tripped her trigger in a way she'd never experienced. Maybe she could enjoy herself—just this once.

Then again, did she really have the strength to resist such a sinfully sexy man, especially when he lured her with an offer to fulfill her secret exhibitionism fantasy? He made her feel sexual, made her believe that he understood her. Admitting that fact was uncomfortable, but even when Ali annoyed her, he turned her on. Maybe the chemistry between them was worth exploring.

And maybe she was out of her mind.

Crossing the room, Shanna was conscious of male eyes following her. God, why had Alejandro sent her this sheer halter top, held in place by nothing more than two little bows, along with a matching wrap-around skirt? Why had he insisted she wear a skimpy outfit in shades of soft creamy-gold that blended in with her skin?

"Hi," a voice whispered in her ear. She turned to find a guy with dimples and incredible blue eyes visually eating her up. "Dance?"

Okay, he was attractive. Who was she kidding? He was gorgeous. The way he looked at her made her burn. But to dance with him? Touch him? Hmm. The thought of getting physical with this guy— with most any guy—wasn't quite as tempting. For her, it was always that way.

Except with Alejandro.

"I—I..."

"She's spoken for tonight."

Alejandro. She recognized that deep, slightly accented voice caressing the back of her neck. And the tingle that shimmied up her spine when he wrapped his arm around her bare midriff in a gesture designed to lay his claim.

Dimples shot her a brief look of regret. "Sure, Mr. Diaz."

"She'll be around later, in the chrome room."

That information perked Dimples up. He raked her with a lingering glance. "Sweet. I'll definitely be watching."

Before Shanna could protest, Alejandro urged her forward, to an employees-only entrance, and shut the door behind them. The decibel level went down about a thousand percent.

She whirled to face him "You *invited* him to watch us?"

Shanna was glad she'd managed to parlay her shock into actual words quickly. Because once she saw his casual black shirt unbuttoned all the way down the front, exposing a healthy glimpse of hard-steel pecs and smooth bronze skin, she lost her train of thought.

"Yes, I did. He is one of the newer regulars and he was here last week. Think of him as a potential suspect."

His voice brought her gaze back up to his face, where a hint of a smile played. The bastard knew she'd been staring at his chest.

She needed dispassion, not lust. *Focus.* "He had no idea who I was. No concept that I'm Kristoff's partner."

"Not that he let on. But if he was guilty, why would he tip his hand?"

Good question. One for which she had no answer.

"You are not required to play this scene. Do you want to change your mind?"

He was wrong; she was absolutely required to play this scene, at least if she wanted to win the competition and hold that trophy in her hand after sixteen years of hard work. But that wasn't the only reason. If she wanted to find out if Alejandro had been right about her desire to exhibit, she had to go through with this. And if she wanted to know if she could actually feel pleasure in this man's arms... Well, then she couldn't chicken out.

"Just lead the way."

With a slow nod, Ali grabbed her hand and gave it a reassuring squeeze, then led her down the hall. Despite her nerves, Shanna had a hard time ripping her gaze from his tight ass, displayed so mouth-wateringly in black slacks. The view alone made her want to jump him. That had to stop. This sexual hunger wasn't like her. Being too into him wasn't a good idea, either. She wasn't into flings, and a guy who co-owned a club like *Sneak Peek* probably wasn't into relationships.

Tearing her gaze away and focusing on her surroundings, she noticed they filed past some open doors containing offices brimming with computers manned by staff members. A wall clock said it was ten `til nine.

The butterflies in her stomach were head-banging and had set up a rave. She wondered if she was going to throw up before she and Alejandro got started.

He stopped in front of a door. "Relax. You will be fine. We're going to handle this together."

"Why are you being nice about this?"

He cocked a brow, the strong angles of his face dusted by shadow and stubble. The frankly sexual stare he sent her made Shanna suck in her breath.

"Certainly, it has not escaped your notice that I want you."

How could it when the thought thrilled her so much? She shook her head.

"Good. I also want to catch the scum taking advantage of our members. You want to catch him, too, so Kristoff's video doesn't fall into the judges' hands. It is a win-win for us both."

"Is that the only reason?"

He shook his head. "I suspect you're not the untouchable bitch you wish me—and everyone else—to believe you are." He shot her a wolfish grin. "But I intend to find out tonight for sure. Personally, I think we will be very hot together."

Before she could protest and slap up the armor he'd verbally stripped away, he thrust the door open and walked through.

They entered the room she had observed the Master and Slut use yesterday. Only things had changed. The chrome bed had been pushed to one corner, at the edge of the stage. The rest of the furniture had been moved out, leaving a large amount of the painted concrete floor well lit and totally empty. The bedding had changed as well. Luxurious white and silvery linens with fluffy pillows dotted with beads and tassels decorated the bed, looking sumptuous on top of the downy blanket. A far cry from yesterday's stark black sheets.

"What's this?"

"I thought you would be more comfortable if we changed the room up to something softer. Something more...you."

Normally, she would protest his judgment that she was soft. But he was right; the look of the room did reflect her more. She wondered how much of her he already saw.

Against her better judgment, she was touched. "Thank you."

"You are very welcome. Come with me." Alejandro tugged her to the edge of the stage. Deep in gray shadows, she saw a lone, imposing figure.

"Hi, Shanna."

"Del?"

"Yes. We're ready to go. How are you doing?"

She resisted the urge to press a hand against her fluttering belly. It would reveal too much, make her look vulnerable. She already felt too much that way for comfort. "Fine."

"Good. The security cameras have been positioned to watch the audience, specifically the corner in which we think the last video was made. The lighting in the audience is a bit brighter, so the cameras can capture whatever is going on. None of the cameras will be pointed at the stage, and Alejandro will take care of you if something unexpected happens. Security is through that door." He pointed to the door without a handle. "Just knock, and they'll let you in immediately."

Wow, they'd thought of everything. "Thank you."

"We will start slow," Alejandro assured her. "Right now, just you and me. Del will watch. As you get comfortable, he'll open the door. Hopefully, your blackmailer will be waiting to get in."

Del watching them. Other strangers staring. Now came the hard part. And the arousing part. She wished the thought of Alejandro touching her didn't turn her on...almost as much as she wished the thought of a crowd seeing their every move didn't make her blood race.

But it all did. Unbearably. And Ali knew it.

Shanna bit her lip. "O-okay."

"Good." Alejandro smiled, something that both set her at ease and made her heart trip. In one look, he managed to both calm her fears and rouse her body.

Shanna couldn't shake the feeling this night would be unlike anything she could possibly have imagined.

She glanced at Del. He was a big shape sitting in the dark corner, his head cocked, his arms crossed over his chest.

"Focus on me, *querida*," Alejandro murmured. "Only me."

She gave him a shaky nod, and he tugged on the hand he was holding, pulling her body into his.

"Dance with me."

"D-dance?"

He nodded. "Just dance."

After a quick snap of his fingers, music filtered through the room, a soft but spicy Latin tune, perfect for a rumba. In fact, it was the music they had danced to just a few nights before.

As Alejandro led her into a basic, her body brushing his with every step, her feet moved automatically to the beat. His unbuttoned shirt fluttered as he moved, offering tantalizing glimpses of hard pectorals, flat, brown nipples, hints of dark hair. Her mind whirled with possibilities.

"You recall the exact music we danced to the other night?"

"I never forget a thing about you."

She melted—on the spot. No man had ever taken such an interest in just her, been so keenly attentive.

Shanna relaxed against him and drifted into the dance. He sensed it and spiced up their steps. After a sharp turn in his arms, her nearly bare back rested against his half-covered chest, his hot breath on her neck, her hips gyrating against his erection. His palm flattened against her naked belly, which flared hot with arousal at his hot touch.

She turned her head, glancing over her shoulder at him. His fiery gaze was full of challenge as he slowly caressed her until both of his hands came rested on her hips. Then he guided them in a movement that was pure, raw sex.

"Del is watching us. Watching you. Getting hard for you," he whispered.

"No," she protested automatically.

But her blood flashed hot at the thought.

Alejandro turned her out in a sharp spin and brought her crashing into his body again, then into a deep dip.

Her gaze snapped up to his. His face loomed dominant, masterful. "Yes."

Her nipples went hard.

As he brought her up slowly, he curled one hand around her nape. The other he flattened between her breasts...before slowly shifting to press over one soft mound. He teased her nipple with a soft touch.

Shanna sucked in a breath. Desire dropped like a bomb into the pit of her stomach. That strong face of his—all hint of teasing, of reassuring, of politeness—gone. In his place stood a man who meant to have her.

While he fitted his hips against hers and rocked, his lips collided with hers. A brush, a slide, a taste. Shanna followed his lead, shocked at the way her heart accelerated like a race car's, zooming to hyper-speed in seconds until it pounded in her ears. He tasted of coffee and man and aggression. She opened to him, aching for him to sink deeper.

Instead, he spun her out. She whirled away from him on instinct.

The rumba was the dance of love...but there was teasing involved. The woman hesitating, the man pursuing. Somehow she knew Alejandro loved to pursue.

The last thing she should do was make her surrender too easy for him.

She walked away, hips swaying, head held high. For a moment, she focused on Del. He leaned forward in his chair, his posture tense. His fingers clutched the chair in front of him. She smiled, writhed, and caressed her way between her breasts, down her belly, skirting her aching sex to caress the tops of her thighs. She heard Del's indrawn breath when the music paused.

Feminine power, heady and amazing, crashed into her. This was why she loved dancing, knowing she could make men want, people feel, just by watching her body.

Then she glanced over her shoulder as Alejandro prowled closer, shedding his black shirt, leaving it forgotten on the floor, as he neared. Powerful bronze shoulders snagged her gaze. His hard-muscled chest narrowed into six-pack abs dusted with a treasure trail that disappeared into the waistband of his pants. The enticing view made her mouth water. But the look on his face...hungry, unrepentant, demanding, made her shudder with want.

Damn, she was staring—and loving it.

Alejandro stopped directly behind her, so close she could feel the heat of his body. Even though he didn't touch her, he sucked her deeper into his sexual web just by being near and sharing the rhythm of the dance.

Suddenly...a tug, a brush of his fingers. The little halter top fell to the floor at her feet.

Leaving her naked from the waist up.

Instinctively, she reached up to cover her breasts with her hands. Alejandro slid his palms down her arms, skin to skin, until his hands covered hers. He rocked against her ass, his erection insistent at her lower back. He planted teasing kisses down her neck, across her shoulder.

Tension tightened in her belly. Resistance melted.

Then he forced her hands down, over her ribs, down her belly, right over her swollen, aching folds. His hips swiveled to the music, moving hers in time—grinding her clit into her fingertips.

"Jesus," Del muttered from the audience.

His voice slammed through Shanna's head. Sensation exploded. She gasped as a riot of feelings tore through her, leaving fire in its wake. Her knees melted. Her head fell back to Alejandro's bare shoulder. Her eyes closed as she moaned.

One of his hands swept across her abdomen again, soft, slow... inching up, up... Until Alejandro claimed her bare breast, his palm burning her sensitive flesh.

Del watched their every move, his gaze riveted to Alejandro's hand moving over her skin. Shanna knew Del saw her arousal, knew he wasn't missing the fact she was spiked up on need and desire.

Aching. And it only climbed higher, knowing that Del couldn't peel his eyes away.

Her nipple poked Alejandro's palm. She arched into his hand as his thumb teased the hard tip.

"Touch me," she whispered.

"Every last inch of you." Alejandro's mouth strung a fresh line of shiver-inducing kisses up her neck.

Suddenly, he grabbed one of her hands, twirled her out, then reeled her back in, her chest crushed to his. Slowly, he eased her away in a rumba rhythm.

His hazel eyes flared as he drank in his first clear glimpse of her bare breasts.

"Such hard, pink nipples. I'm going to enjoy making them red."

Her heart all but stopped before pounding again. "H-how? By pinching them?"

He reached between their bodies and slid blistering palms over her breasts. His thumbs cradled their aching tips as his fingers closed in and pressed, jolting her with a flash of pain, followed by a haze of pleasure.

"That is one way."

"And b-by sucking them?"

His gaze was like an inferno burning her up as he dipped her back over his arm, arching her breasts toward his mouth, fusing their hips together. God, she could feel every inch of his thick erection pressing right against her sex. She ached in a way she never had before and never believed she could.

Then he lowered his head and sucked her nipple into his mouth.

Hot. Wet. Wild. Thrilling. Sensations screamed through her body as he suckled her, his mouth pulling, tugging, creating friction that zipped right from her breast to her clit until pleasure tightened, converged, pounded at her body.

Shanna clutched his shoulders, praying the sensation would never end.

After a long, lingering lick, Alejandro eased away from her breast and stood her upright again. "That is another possibility."

"Do you... W-would you bite them?"

He didn't even answer, just bent to capture her breast in his mouth again, the hot silk of his tongue over the sensitive bud giving way to the tug of teeth—and a bolt of pure fire straight down to her sex.

Oh god.

"Yes!" The word slipped out of her mouth. Surrender in one syllable. She knew it. So did he.

She was going to give him anything—everything—he wanted tonight.

Alejandro straightened and smiled down at her. That expression captured her, but he enthralled her when he slid his fingers into her hair, scattering the pins holding her French twist everywhere, and ravaged her mouth.

Need, impatience, aggression, the promise of unbelievable sex—it was all there in his kiss. His tongue stroked hers and stoked the fires licking inside her, sending her higher and higher.

Alejandro had barely touched anything below her waist and already she felt screamingly close to orgasm. He'd already brought her closer to the pinnacle than any of her other previous lovers. Damn, what would happen if—when?—he laid her down on that sumptuous bed and covered her body with his? When he filled her up with every inch he taunted her with even now as he rocked against her?

Panting, mewling, Shanna grabbed his face with clutching fingers and pressed her lips harder against his. God, it was stupid and dangerous...and she ached to find out just how good he really was.

5

*S*hanna panted, clinging to Alejandro when he lodged his thigh between hers and urged her to swivel her hips against him.

Thick bolts of need speared her belly, slicing down her legs. Her blood turned thick. The wanton within her demanded more.

She wasn't the Bitch of the Ballroom tonight. She was just a female surrendering to the hot sensations her lover's touch roused. How it happened, she didn't know. Why now and with this man, in this situation, was a mystery, too. But for once, she felt like a woman. Not just an athlete, a dancer, or a competitor. Just a woman in touch with her sexuality.

Orgasm approached hard and fast. Tension built between her legs. Heat fractured her thoughts. She moaned, feeling Alejandro's hands at her hips, urging her on, and Del's hot stare burning her back.

As she climbed up, up, Alejandro lifted his mouth from hers and sent her a deliciously wicked smile. God, the man could melt steel with that look. And she was nowhere near that solid.

"You ache." He didn't ask; he stated.

"Yes."

"You are wet."

No doubt, he felt her wet folds through the thin fabric of his slacks, and the friction it provided was driving her out of her mind.

"Yes."

Then he reached around her, lifted her skirt to her waist , and gliding rough palms over her bare ass. Shanna knew Del could see her cheeks and the delicate white thong bisecting them. She swore she could feel his stare burning her backside. And she knew it affected him because he groaned.

That sound reached between her legs and jolted her. Why it turned her on so much to turn Del on she couldn't explain. And she didn't want to know. Tomorrow, she'd likely be mortified. Tonight, she just didn't care.

"Do you like knowing that Del is eating up your ass with his hungry gaze?" Ali rasped in her ear. "That he's so hard for you and would kill to be in my place right now?"

Shanna couldn't help it; she whimpered.

"That's right. But he will not touch you. He will watch and he will want, but *I* will take every sinful pleasure your body has to offer."

The man knew how to talk to her. With a few choice words, he utterly unwound her.

Then he tugged on the tie securing the skirt around her waist and , slipped the last button free. Her skirt fluttered to the stage. Now she wore nothing but her very damp thong.

He lowered his hands to her hips again, forcing her sex down on his thigh once more. To the music, they swayed, h=is impressive erection brushing her belly, inciting more hunger. Her need to come grew, expanded until she was moaning, muttering words of nonsense and need.

"Please. Please!"

"I will give you all you can take. Then, *querida*, I will give you more."

He barely finished whispering the promise when he bent her

back over his arm, arching her breasts up so he could feast on them again. Her nipples were so hard under his tongue, and no matter how he licked, suckled, bit, she only wanted more.

To be so lost in the moment, in the sensation, stunned and amazed Shanna. For all the times she'd wondered if she was "normal" because she didn't respond to a man's touch, she now had her answer. She responded to Alejandro. To Del standing now, his eyes on her. To the forbidden burn of everything they night transpire tonight.

Still bent over Alejandro's arm, Shanna locked her stare with Del's, to entice him with what he couldn't have. And though the room was upside down from this vantage, she could not miss the small crowd filing in. Men. More than five, less than a dozen, they all had tense bodies, hot eyes.

"Fuck, she's hot," murmured a total stranger.

Del stood in the middle of them, fists clenched at his sides. "She is that."

"They want you," Alejandro murmured against her neck. "And I want to show them what they're missing."

Before she could even process what he meant, Alejandro spun her around to face the audience. Oh, God, they stood a mere three feet away. So close she swore she could feel their hot breaths on her skin. She recognized Dimples there. His smile was gone, replaced by seething want and an erection a blind woman couldn't miss.

He and the rest of the crowd were focused on her bare breasts, loose and heavy as Ali forced her hips to maintain the rhythm of the music.

Collective groans resounded, sending a rush of desire inside her. Could she actually come simply from being watched?

Since she frequently had trouble orgasming during masturbation, simply letting loose here, now, was a heady, wonderful thought.

Then Alejandro slid his palms down her arms, still behind her, rocking to the beat of the music. Then he grasped her wrists and lifted her hands above her head until they encircled his neck.

Another chorus of groans erupted from the audience. A quick glance down proved the new pose raised her breasts, made her nipples stand straight out like an invitation.

"Don't move," Alejandro commanded. "Just feel...and let go."

She gave him a shaky nod, wondering, eager—aching—for whatever he planned next.

Shanna didn't have to wait long. A moment later, his fingertips trailed down the side of her breast, across the flat of her abdomen, and disappeared right into her tiny wet thong.

He gave her no time to absorb the fact he was fondling her in public—and that she loved it—before his fingers zeroed in on her clit. A brush, a rub. An electric spark. Tingles danced through her sex, in her belly, down her thighs. The tension ratcheted up until she could barely breathe.

"You going to come for them?" Ali whispered in her ear.

She nodded erratically.

"You going to come for me?"

"Yes!" She bit her lip to keep from screaming as the ache deepened into something nearly unbearable.

With the music throbbing in her ears, Alejandro's fingers shoving her past the breaking point, with nearly a dozen sets of hot male eyes and thoughts enveloped in only her, Shanna came apart.

Her hoarse cry erupted above the music. Her eyes closed, and pleasure washed over her, sharp, golden, unbelievable.

Nothing had ever been like that. Nothing had ever prepared her for the addicting rush of pure sensation lighting up her body. *Oh. My. God.*

Alejandro took her down slowly before extracting his hand from her panties. When he did, she looked down to find his fingers saturated with her cream.

He gave a satisfied chuckle in her ear. "This is how I want you, soaked for me."

She gasped as he anointed her nipples with her juice, then whirled her to face him. With long, languid swipes of his tongue, he licked her taste away with a moan that reverberated deep inside her, stirring the ache back to life.

Shanna was shocked when he stepped away and took her hand in his. Suddenly, she was aware of being almost totally bare, while everyone around her was half clothed or more. She *felt* naked. Vulnerable. Yet oddly strong. She glanced between Alejandro and the tense, shuffling audience.

"That's it?"

He leaned in, looking to the world like a lover planting soft kisses just below her ear. "If you want it to be. We certainly gave the blackmailer something to film."

Yes, but was it enough? And was that really the reason she was contemplating the words about to come out of her mouth?

"I want more."

Alejandro glanced down into her face, his stare delving deep into hers. "Are you sure?"

All she knew was that she wasn't ready for tonight to end. She nodded.

Gently, he grabbed her wrist and placed her hand over his erection. Damn, he was hard. And very large. *Oh, wow...*

"I'm dying to feel you around me," he whispered. "Your mouth, your pussy... Tell me what you want. How much of you will you give me?"

The real question was, could she actually hold anything back?

Shanna felt her way up his cock, to the catch of his slacks. She flipped it open, and he sucked in a harsh breath. Another groan from the audience spurred her on. With slow torture in mind, she eased down his zipper, taking her sweet time.

"If you have a 'no' on the tip of your tongue, say it now."

Shanna leaned closer to his primal male heat, her mouth hovering above the hard nub of his brown nipple. She flicked a sultry gaze up to his face, latching onto his burning stare. "Never heard the word."

When had she ever been brazen? Or assertive or hungry or dying to feel a man's animal heat burning her up? Never. For years, she'd poured her passion into dance. When she performed, she could express all her pent-up feelings through the movements of her body and the interaction with her partner. In real life...she'd never put a tenth of her passion into sex. Tonight—now—she wanted to change all that.

Alejandro had compelled her to.

She closed her mouth around his nipple and nibbled him with her teeth. He groaned long and loud. Holding in her satisfied smile, she pushed his pants over his hips, sliding them down his thighs.

His sex sprang free, so hard it nearly lay against his belly. So long, it reached toward his navel. So thick, she could barely get her hand all the way around it. So perfect, she knew that once he sank deep into her, she'd feel not only more pleasure she'd ever experienced, but ecstasy beyond her wildest fantasies.

Panting, Shanna fell to her knees. She could hardly wait.

~

*W*hen his slacks reached his ankles, Alejandro was very glad he hadn't bothered with anything underneath.

He was even more glad to see Shanna on her knees, eyeing his cock.

Alejandro took himself in hand and guided the weeping head closer to the red haven of her lush mouth.

He barely anchored his palm around the crown of her head when she opened wide to take inch after inch inside the stunning, wet heat as she cradled him on her tongue. *Dios mío!*

She sucked hard, and he felt her all over his cock. His head nudged the back of her throat. Her tongue swiped the sensitive underside of his erection, swirled around the purple crest.

Heaven—Shanna had to be it. She was definitely sleek and built for long, sweaty, intense fucks—and to show off for the audience that would masturbate to the sight and sounds of her.

About that, he had no doubt.

To his left, the audience watched. Moaned. A few guys were adjusting themselves. Others had given up and were already stroking their own cocks. A few women had wandered into the room, and he hoped they understood there would likely be a long line to fuck them if they stayed.

Then Shanna drew back, her tongue laving the head of his cock, igniting a maelstrom of icy-hot tingles in his balls, down his spine. He stopped thinking completely. Too full of sensation now, he fucked her mouth slowly as she whimpered around him, her fingers locked on his thighs...slowly inching up to his ass.

She took him to the back of her throat again. Her nails dug into his skin, and the hint of pain pushed him closer to the edge of pleasure. Damn, he was going to come if she kept that up.

A part of him wanted to rush into the ache and explode on her tongue, down her throat, just for the joy of watching her take and swallow him.

But he wanted to fuck her more. Way more.

Gritting his teeth, Ali pulled out of her mouth. She protested with an unintelligible groan, but he bent and grabbed her waist, lifting her until she stood. Then he whirled her away from him, to face the tall, chrome bed poster. He forced her to bend toward it, then with his fingers over hers, he clasped her hands around the pole.

"Hold on. You will need to," he growled in her ear.

Bending quickly, he found the condom in his pocket and rolled it on, counting the torturous heartbeats until he could be balls deep in the sweet heat of her pussy. Seven seconds. That's all it took until he gripped her hips and thrust inside her.

Scalding hot. Fist tight. *Madre de Dios*, he wasn't going to last. But by damn, she was going over the edge first.

Bracketing harsh fingers on her hips, he pushed his way inside. Shoved hard. It seemed to take forever. Her pussy was so swollen, and if he had to guess, she had not had sex in months, maybe longer.

That was going to change. No way would tonight be the last time he fucked her. No way would he wait weeks, or even days, to feel her again. Even waiting hours sounded doubtful in that moment.

Jacked up on an overload of sensation and a burning need to come brewing at the base of his spine, Ali took a deep breath and plunged into her slowly. Hell, it wasn't helping his concentration to see people masturbating to the sight of Shanna's naked body. Or one of the women in the room with her skirt around her waist and a man's cock buried inside her as she straddled his lap.

Tearing his gaze away, he focused on the long line of Shanna's graceful spine, her mussed golden tresses spilling across her narrow back. He couldn't *not* touch her.

Lifting one hand off her hip, he reached around her body and toyed with her breasts, pinching one of her responsive nipples. She gasped, and Alejandro felt his primitive side take over. He sank his teeth into her neck. He squeezed her other nipple. Her body responded instinctively, tightening on his cock. She was close.

Thank god. So was he.

Gliding his palm down her belly, he buried his fingers into the sparse curls between her legs. *There.* Her clit stood up, hard and swollen, pleading for attention. He wasn't about to say no.

He swiped his fingers across her bundle of nerves. She moaned, tightened again. The friction of moving inside her was about to blow the top off his head. But he kept moving.

"Do you see them watching you?" he snarled, on the edge. "Do you see them wanting you?"

"Yes," she cried. "Yes."

"I want you more."

"Oh, god," she gasped. "Alejandro!"

He strummed her clit once more. "You are going to come."

Damn, he was trying so hard to hold it together, he was cross-eyed and slurring his words. But she understood.

"Yes!"

And then she did, crying out as she clamped down on him, massaging his cock with the pulsing walls of her sex. His self-control didn't stand a chance.

The sensation started deep in his gut and dropped with heavy need right into his balls. Pleasure climbed up, up, up his cock until he found himself shouting his throat raw in release.

He clutched her tight, pumping his way through utopia, with just one thought rattling through his fevered brain:

Mine.

6

*L*atin music throbbed—kind of like Shanna's head. The insistent beat of the dramatic notes echoed off the hardwood floors and bounced off the mirrored walls of the studio. Her feet ached. She was hot and sweaty after three hours. And really annoyed. She and Kristoff were *not* having a productive practice.

And as much as she hated to admit it, Alejandro kept invading her thoughts every three seconds. How could she miss him so much after a mere two days? Why couldn't she stop thinking about the way his hands felt on her, of his unique scent like midnight and man all wrapped in pure sex. Why hadn't she stopped remembering the way he'd looked at her—as if she meant something—before she thrust her clothes on and darted out of his embrace? It would be far more practical if she could focus on the fact that the security cameras hadn't picked up on anything suspicious that night at *Sneak Peek*, so she was no closer to finding—and stopping—the blackmailer.

"I have never had to say this to you," Kristoff broke into her thoughts, "but if we are going to win, you must concentrate. You know this, yes? The cha-cha-cha, it is strong and passionate, not lethargic and distracted."

Damn Kristoff for stepping on her last nerve.

Shanna thrust her hands on her hips. "If I'm distracted, it's because I'm still trying to figure out how we're going to keep that porn-worthy footage of yours out of the judges' hands. And guess what? The fact that's even a problem is not my fault."

"I made a mistake. I have apologized. Either forgive me or find a new partner. Or have you already been having auditions behind my back?"

In the past, that comment alone would have been enough to push her over the edge. She would have told Kristoff to spend his time at *Sneak Peek* and stop wasting hers. Then she would have begun auditioning partners the very same day.

So why wasn't she walking away now?

Kristoff was, in a word, amazing. A powerful dancer, determined, dedicated. He brought a glamour to their dancing that had been lacking with Jonathan. The ladies loved him. He oozed charm even when making his matador face during the paso doble. He was spirited, and normally, he made practice fun. And yes, she wanted to find a partner with whom she could finish her career.

That wasn't why she didn't want to lose Kristoff, though. During their time together, he'd become...almost a friend. She tried very hard not to bring her emotions into her dance partnerships, but Shanna knew he hadn't intended to make a mess of things. She hated the thought of turning her back on him and proving his suspicions about her right.

In the past, it had never bothered her to be known as the Bitch of the Ballroom. Now, for some reason...it bothered her. A lot.

"Shut up and dance," she snapped.

"We can still win."

They could, if they didn't have that footage hanging over their heads. But why bring it up again? It wouldn't change their situation. Still, she usually would have added the dig just to remind him exactly how he'd screwed up. Today, she didn't have petty in her, not when there was a bit of kicked puppy in his expression.

Damn it, had the handful of orgasms Alejandro had given her softened her that much? Shanna stiffened her spine. She couldn't afford to think with her heart if she wanted to win. And winning was all she had, even if it sounded...empty.

No, she was just tired or something. She'd worked too hard to lose focus now. If she couldn't figure out who was behind this blackmail before the competition, she would likely have to cut Kristoff loose.

"We can win if we keep that video out of circulation. I'm working on that."

"Is that why you went to *Sneak Peek* and performed a public scene with Alejandro Diaz?"

Shanna nearly choked. It hadn't occurred to her that Kristoff would find out. In retrospect, she should have known. He was a member. She hadn't seen him there, but clearly someone had told him.

He laughed. "I heard it was very hot and that you had a rapt audience."

"I did what needed to be done to lure our blackmailer."

Or had she really done whatever she had to in order to achieve those stunning pair of orgasms. She'd barely resisted Alejandro's offer of a third, which he'd promised to give her in his bed, just the two of them on soft satin sheets.

"And you did it very well, I hear."

Shanna rolled her eyes and turned away so he wouldn't see her cheeks turning pink.

But she wasn't fast enough.

"You're blushing. You?" Astonishment laced Kristoff's voice. "I have never seen you do such a thing."

It was rare, and all because Alejandro had blown her away, and she hadn't recovered yet. She had never craved sex or ached for any man. Until him. Last night, before she'd lost herself in the sensations of self-pleasure while thinking of Ali, she'd wondered exactly what he had done to her and why she was so fascinated by him.

How had he gotten under her skin so quickly?

Pretending to walk across the studio nonchalantly, Shanna sought her bottle of water and drank deep, then turned back to Kristoff. "Apparently, our plan wasn't good enough. We didn't catch anyone in the act of filming us, as we'd hoped. No one has sent me another blackmail video or threatened me as a result of the whole thing." She shrugged. "I guess it was a waste of time."

But it didn't feel like a waste, given what he'd done next...

After the scene had ended, Alejandro had pressed a button to drop a partition between them and the audience. Shanna heard the watchers filing out, which filled her with a sense of both loss and relief. Then he had turned her to face him and taken her into his arms. For a simple hug. He'd said not a word, asked for nothing else for long moments. He just held her, stroked her hair. She hadn't had that in a long time. Years. Her father and brothers certainly never gave affection. And she had needed it even more than she'd realized.

Shanna had clenched her eyes shut tightly, resisting an urge to crawl deeper into his embrace and cry for all the fear—and conversely, the bliss—soaking her body. In the aftermath of their sex, her emotions had tumbled, jumbled, whirled all around. Up was down, backward was forward; nothing made sense except holding onto him.

Somehow, she'd managed to restrain her tears, tear herself from his arms, and reach for her clothes.

Within minutes, Del emerged into the room with the unhappy news that security had been scouring the footage of the event and found no one in the audience with a camera of any kind.

After Del left, Shanna had lost it. Tears had fallen hard and fast. But silently. She'd hoped Alejandro had noticed.

Wishful thinking.

"Don't cry," he'd whispered as he swooped her up into his arms.

She'd been too weak to fight Alejandro, especially when he'd felt so strong while he'd settled her against his solid body and in the shelter of his arms. As he'd kissed his way down her face, he'd been so tender, as if he'd known exactly what she needed. He'd ripped right through her fragile barriers. She'd opened up to his whispered words and tender mouth...

Then he'd taken her hand and led her out of the main house,

down a pathway hidden by tropical plants and climbing ivy, softly lit by the full moon, then pushed his way toward a luxurious cottage.

His private quarters.

Being alone with him when she was so emotionally raw...not smart. Downright scary, in fact. Even the idea had made her heart skid, her palms go clammy.

Clutching her keys, Shanna had mumbled something about a fictitious early-morning practice and fled.

So, it was done. They were done. Now, she needed to get her mind off of the repeated messages he'd left since and focus on dancing. She had the biggest competition of her career to prepare for. He had a business to run. Why he continued to pursue her, she had no idea. They had nothing in common.

Except great sex.

"Earth to Shanna," Kristoff joked. "Are you with me?"

"Yes. Sorry. I have a headache." That wasn't a lie actually...just not the whole truth.

"Sorry. What should we do next about...the problem? Perhaps you should seek out a new partner."

He looked so sad at the prospect. Something in her chest twinged, and she tried to shove it aside, but that wasn't working.

"We don't have time to talk about this now. You have to be at work in two hours, and I have to meet with the costumer shortly. Let's focus on today."

"It would not hurt you to talk to me. Do you want to talk about what happened at *Sneak Peek*?"

As her brothers would say, *oh, hell no.* "Talking won't win us any trophies. From the top."

Using the remote control, she started the music again and got into position. Sighing, Kristoff assumed his pose and they danced for another grueling half hour.

Until the door to the studio swung open unexpectedly.

Alejandro strolled in looking dark and yummy and like a man with an agenda—one that started with getting her out of her clothes.

Shanna sucked in a breath. "What are you doing here?"

"I assume your phone is broken, since you have not returned my calls." He arched a brow. "So I decided to find you."

"We're practicing."

The protest was automatic. His presence here, so unexpected, raised her defenses. Thank god. She needed those barriers against him. If she spent another hour with the man, feeling as weak as she had while he touched her, she'd collapse against him and... Shanna shivered. She'd be vulnerable to him, probably admit that she cared.

Not acceptable.

"You will win because we will uncover who has been blackmailing you," Alejandro vowed.

"The security tapes turned up nothing, you said."

"That is true. And I assume the blackmailer has not contacted you, or you would have let me know."

"Yes, I would have." And she would, no matter how much talking to him would have tempted her to do more—the way she wanted to right now. "But I haven't received anything so far. So we have nothing else to say."

Alejandro's expression told he her could see right through her bluster and wasn't put off in the least. Damn him! Why couldn't he cringe, like most people?

"How did you find out when and where we were practicing?" she demanded.

With a sweep of his hand, Alejandro outted Kristoff as the culprit.

She whirled on her partner angrily. "This is practice time, not social hour. What the hell were you thinking?"

"That if I did not tell him how to find you, he would end my privileges at *Sneak Peek*."

Shanna gritted her teeth. Fabulous. Yet another example of a man thinking with his penis. Apparently, it had never occurred to him—or he didn't care—that she hadn't wanted Alejandro to find her.

"I have been thinking," Kristoff said. "Since your first effort to draw the blackmailer did not solve the problem that you should try again."

"Are you serious?" Her jaw dropped.

Kristoff nodded. "Stage another public scene. The word about it is out now. People in the community are buzzing about you two. If you give advance warning, I believe the person responsible will come."

Shanna considered Kristoff's words with dread—and excitement. More of Alejandro's touches, his wild sort of lovemaking... So very tempting. She hadn't just liked what they'd done together; she had basked in it. And had been aching for more since.

Not a good idea. More Alejandro would only addict her further to the man. And while she didn't know him well, she doubted he would settle for a woman whose schedule was as demanding as hers, especially since she spent nearly every day dancing in very suggestive ways with another man. Besides, she'd bet Alejandro would expect a great deal emotionally from the woman he called his—certainly more than she was comfortable giving. He had to see her limitations.

So why was he still pursuing her?

As much as she'd like to give into her fears and dismiss Alejandro, what Kristoff said made sense. Maybe the blackmailer had not acted last time because he hadn't known about the scene. Or been able to be there that night. She and Alejandro had done little to spread the word beforehand. The audience who had witnessed her coming apart in Ali's arms had largely been there by chance.

"I agree," Alejandro said. "I want to catch this bastard. But the choice is Shanna's."

She bit her lip. With the competition in three days, her options were running thin. Throwing away almost twenty years of training, sweating, and suffering to avoid having sex with Alejandro seemed beyond stupid, even if fear screamed that she should run like hell.

Reluctantly, Shanna nodded. "I'll be there tonight."

Alejandro shook his head. "Tomorrow night. Give me time to suggest that there may be a repeat performance, just in case the scum does not have his ear to the ground, so to speak."

Shanna released the breath she didn't realize she'd been holding. She wanted desperately to be with him. At the same time, she didn't. It was so unlike her to be indecisive and conflicted. She had to regain balance, get a grip on her control.

"Fine," she announced. "I will be there at eight. We'll commence at eight-thirty. I need to be home by ten."

Turning away with a dismissive whirl, she reached for the remote control, intent on starting the music, resuming practice...and ignoring Alejandro before he noticed her trembling and made her completely insane with those hungry stares of his.

Instead, he grabbed her arm and turned her back to face him. "You will be there at eight-thirty. We will commence at nine. If it takes a whole night of public performances, you will stay until we know who and what we are dealing with."

She jerked from his grasp. "Don't presume to tell me what to do."

"Shanna, can you really afford to be impractical and put on your bitch armor with me?"

No.

"I know that is not you," he murmured. "I seek only to help you."

Still, she raised her chin, refusing to back down. "Whatever. If it amuses you to play the caveman—"

"It does not." He leaned close and whispered for her ears only, "But it intrigues me to see you hide from me and the pleasure you know I am going to give you when I have you naked and under me again."

~

*H*ours later, Shanna had showered, changed, and run errands. Life was normal...and yet she was still both seething and overheated by Alejandro's arrogant comments. How could the man manage to irritate and arouse her in a single sentence? For that matter, why did he always incite conflict inside her?

Argh! She needed to forget him.

Her doorbell rang. She wasn't expecting anyone. Probably someone trying to sell her something, maybe Girl Scout cookies. One of the neighbor kids had been selling them yesterday, and the thought of indulging in mindless sugar perked her up.

Shanna opened the door.

Someone stood on the other side, all right. It sure wasn't a Girl Scout.

"Alejandro." His name slipped out as a whisper.

"Good evening, *querida*."

When he murmured that endearment, she melted. Every time. "Don't call me that."

"It bothers you when I call you darling? Why?"

"I am not your darling. We are working together to solve a common problem."

"We are. But I fail to see how that must be the end of it."

Shanna opened her mouth to set him straight, but Alejandro cut her off. "Though I am sure you will invent some reason, but for now, let's not argue. I came to talk."

With narrowed eyes, she tried to gauge his sincerity. "Just talk?"

"Nothing more."

She didn't quite believe him, but he'd roused her curiosity. What could he possibly have to say to her?

"All right. Come in." She stepped back to admit him.

Alejandro shook his head and held out his hand. "Come with me."

"Where?"

"It's a surprise."

"Not the club," she warned him.

He shook his head. "Not the club."

Now she was *really* curious.

Sliding into the sandals she kept by the door, she grabbed her purse and keys off the nearby table. "Will it take long?"

"Hot date tonight?"

His words mocked her. As if he knew that she could hardly wrap her mind around her interest in him, much less imagine being attracted to anyone else right now.

"With dreamland, yes. I'm tired."

"And I am here to cheer you up." He held out his hand to her again.

This time she took it and let herself out the door. "Where are we going?"

"The nature of a surprise is that you should be surprised."

"So you won't tell me?"

He shook his head, sending her a dazzling, unrepentant smile as they walked toward the condo complex's parking lot. "That would spoil it."

"You know that annoys me."

"I know you are used to being in control and making all the decisions. A little relaxation will be good for you."

People had been saying that to her for years. Generally, she ignored them.

"That's your opinion."

"And you cannot change it."

"Okay, but you're wrong."

"How about humoring me, then? Pretend."

She rolled her eyes, holding in a smile. He was persistent, if nothing else. "Whatever."

Alejandro sliced her a victorious grin but wisely said nothing more.

When they reached the parking lot, he lifted his key fob and pressed a button. A sleek, black Mercedes convertible, so new it still bore the temporary plates, beeped and flashed its lights a few feet away.

Business at the club must be *very* good to afford the old place that housed their business and four-wheeled trinkets like this.

He assisted her into the car, then rounded the car to the driver's side, and eased in. "My father was a wealthy man."

"What?"

"I saw the way you looked at my car. I believe you had similar thoughts about the club. I am answering your unspoken question. My father was a wealthy man, and he left me his fortune."

"Not your mother?"

He shrugged and started the car. "I am the only part of him my mother will have anything to do with."

"They divorced?"

"In the Catholic church, no. They separated when I was twelve." He backed out of the parking space and steered into the gorgeous summer night.

"Why are you telling me this?"

"You cannot like someone you do not know."

He wanted her to like him?

"My father was a philandering bastard, if you wished to know why they split up. I remember my mother's tears many nights when my father did not come home. They became my tears, too. He acted as if his affairs were both common and acceptable. Perhaps that was so in their generation... Perhaps it was accepted in his native Argentina..."

Alejandro was sharing something so shockingly private with her. Why?

"I do not agree," he stated. "If you speak vows and make a commitment, it should be solid. You should mean those words."

"True." Was he trying to tell her he'd be faithful? Why did he think it mattered to her?

The fact he felt compelled to give her his opinion known unnerved her. But, being honest, it also thrilled her treacherous soft side. Having a man like Ali in her life full time would be wonderful... but distracting. Indulging was *not* an option. Their search for this blackmailing bastard and her need to win the California Dance Star consumed her every thought and waking moment. Her commitment was to winning. Romance would only interfere.

"Take my friendship with Del," he went on. "Del and I met in college. We quickly became friends—both outcasts to some degree, being foreign-exchange students with somewhat poor English here in Los Angeles. We discovered we shared a lot of similar interests and passions.

"So after graduation, we decided to put our degrees to work on something mutually satisfying. Del used his marketing degree and social media skills to spread word of the club and promote it all around. I used my finance degree to secure the funding, run the back end, and invest our profits. We operate in the black, and each year is more profitable than the last. But two years ago, I had the opportunity to sell out my half for triple the amount I paid to get in." He shrugged. "Long ago, I promised Del I would stay in until we were both ready for a change. I declined the opportunity."

"That cost you a lot of money, I'm sure."

"Losing the friendship would have cost me more."

"You can afford to say that; you have your father's money."

"Not so much anymore. I put a fat chunk of it in a trust for my mother. She thinks I set it up with my money. But the bastard owed her more than he could ever repay. I thought this was fitting."

Shanna stared at Alejandro as if seeing him for the first time. In a way, she was. It was hard not to like him when he was protecting his mother and defending his friendships.

A moment later, they stopped in front of a local ice cream shop, quaint and somewhat old-fashioned. In a few hours, after dinner, this place would be crawling with families. But during the dinner hour, it was nearly empty.

"Ice cream?"

"I assume you like it."

"I haven't eaten dinner yet. I was planning to cook before you came over..."

He climbed out of the car and helped her out. "Who needs dinner when there is ice cream?"

"Who doesn't need protein and nutrients? Ice cream isn't a dinner food."

Alejandro slipped an arm around her, and Shanna tried not to melt against the tempting heat of his body. Why did he have to be so damn sexy?

"I will not tell your mother if you won't," he teased.

"My mother died when I was four."

She found herself choking out the words. She shouldn't have opened her mouth; the truth only made her more vulnerable to him. But withholding that fact after he'd confessed all about his past seemed petty.

"I am sorry."

She hung her head. "I don't remember her. I have this...impression of what her laugh was like. I don't even know if it's accurate."

He squeezed her against his side as they approached the counter. "So your father raised you?"

"Along with my brothers. They're all athletes."

"Which is why you are so driven to win." It was a statement, not a question.

"Second place is nothing more than first loser. It's the family motto."

"Ah, this explains so much about you." He turned to the teenager behind the counter. "A scoop of chocolate peanut butter and...raspberry amaretto. Shanna?"

"None for me. I have to fit into my costume—"

"She will have the same."

"I will not!"

"Then pick your favorite flavors."

"You're going to force me to eat ice cream?"

"I am going to help you take a moment away from ambition and enjoy life."

When was the last time she'd done that? Shanna thought back through the weeks, which became months...and quickly turned into years. The realization stunned her.

She hesitated, then caved in. It was ice cream, not a commitment. Tomorrow, she had a grueling practice. She'd work the calories off.

"Chocolate chip cookie dough and French vanilla."

Alejandro paid as other teenagers behind the counter assembled their cones. In moments, they wandered to a little table outside and began licking on ice cream as the sun dropped closer to the horizon, with the California breeze stirring all around them.

After the first taste, Shanna moaned. "This is amazing."

He smiled. "I discovered this place a few years ago. It's part of my weekly ritual."

"Where do you put it?" She eyed his hard body, absolutely no stranger to his rippled abs.

"I make up for it with plenty of cardio and carrots the rest of the week. But life is meant to be lived, no?"

Had she ever really thought about it in that context? "I suppose so."

"You have been a very single-minded woman for many years. Dance has been your focus, your ambition."

"And my passion."

"No one watching you dance would deny that. You are very talented. You know this, right?"

She supposed. Yes, she could dance. When she watched footage of competitions, she knew she held her own in a room full of talented dancers. For the past few years, she even believed she began to shine a bit brighter than them because she practiced harder and wanted it more.

"I'm pleased with my performances."

"This ambition, does it make you happy?"

Happy? An odd question. She didn't enjoy being frustrated by the champion status she had not achieved yet. But she *would* be a champion. Once the trophy was in her hands, life would be very sweet, and the sacrifices she'd made along the way would have been worth it.

All she had to do was get dangerously close to the most tempting man she'd ever met in order to catch her blackmailer.

His question unsettled her. She'd never thought of her life in a happy/unhappy context. It just was. Of course, questioning her life was too easy to do when she had a man like Alejandro in front of her, reminding her of everything she'd been missing.

"Why shouldn't it?" she asked.

"The way that ice cream cone is dripping and the fact I've rarely seen you smile, I suspect you have spent so much time dancing, you are out of practice when it comes to living."

Dancing was life for her. So what if she didn't eat a lot of ice cream? "Why do you care?"

"Because I am a man who would like to see you happy." He brushed tender fingertips across her cheek. "What is the worst thing that could happen if you do not win Saturday night? Or ever?"

Immediately, she rejected the thought. But it was a fair question, one she'd asked herself during long nights when aching muscles, nagging injuries, and loneliness had kept her awake.

"I don't know." She shook her head. "I can't let that happen. Failure is not an option."

"You cannot control what will happen."

Yeah, that's what worried her.

"So what happens if you never win?"

She hated to even think the answer. But to speak it seemed unbearably personal. Yet Alejandro had poured out a part of his soul to her. He had not mocked her when she'd spoken of her mother, the rest of the family, or the origins of her ambitions. She had no reason to hide from him...except that he kept slipping behind her emotional barriers, which scared the hell out of her.

Why couldn't she put distance between them? Why did she even care about his feelings? Normally, she had no problem with pushing people away, but Ali was...different.

"I would feel like a failure," she whispered.

"You would consider yourself a failure, even after everything you have achieved?"

"Probably. My family would think I'm a failure. I have one brother who has been the top decathlete in the world. One has played in the Super Bowl. My father has two gold medals. I can't compete."

"Who asked you to?"

"You'd have to understand my family. For years, my brothers have endlessly tormented me."

He shrugged. "The nature of men and their sisters. Their way of showing affection is to harass you. More manly that way."

It wasn't that simple, and she didn't know how to explain it. "Family aside, I couldn't give up dancing. I *want* to win, more than anything."

"I would not suggest you give up dance. I merely think you should take the floor to indulge your joy of dance, not to pursue a trophy. The journey is the treasure, not the prize at the end."

"Now you're a philosopher?"

Alejandro shook his head and placed a soft kiss against her ice-cream cold lips. "Just a man who wants to see you smile. Will you?"

Shanna looked at Alejandro. He was so comfortable with himself. Somehow wiser than a man who ran a club for sexual indulgences should be. He made everything seem so easy. Even personal discussions, which she usually downright loathed, felt freakishly natural. No pressure. No scolding or telling her how to do things. No taunting her about her failures. Just a steady voice, a tender touch, with lots of insight.

Lovely...but none of that would put a trophy in her hand.

Shanna wrapped her fingers around his and smiled. "There. Are you happy?"

"I have seen more genuine smiles at a beauty pageant."

Sighing, Shanna sat back and licked at her cone. "Really, why does it matter to you if I'm happy?"

Ali paused, seeming to weigh his words. "You matter. I would hate to see you sacrifice everything for something that may never happen. You have given up high school frivolities, friendships, romances...for a hunk of metal and a title."

He was right...and wrong. Being a champion was everything to her.

"This is why I don't date." She stood and glared down at him. "I don't expect you to understand. No one does."

He stood and met her glare. "You have ended more than one dance partnership to pursue winning over friendship. What has that gotten you except a bad reputation? Those partners invested in you, cared about you. You cast them aside."

"I had to! One was so injured, it was clear he was never coming back."

"Might he have tried harder to recover if you had given him both a reason and a partner to return to?"

Guilt sliced through her. Maybe. Likely not...but maybe. Curt had been a hard worker and possessed a drive to win. Last she heard, he was selling insurance.

"Martin dropped me in competition. I could not risk it happening again. I'd lost faith in his ability, and a couple without trust does not function well."

"The drop must have been painful, and I understand why you would not want to partner with someone ill equipped for the job. But as you say, trust is essential. After nearly two years together, you never gave him a chance to rebuild it between you."

She rolled her eyes. "What are you, my dance pimp? And before you start in on Jonathan, that decision was mutual. He wanted to get married more than he wanted to dance."

Surprise flashed across his dark face. "Really? My mother will be happy to hear that. She hates you because you ran off her favorite."

Shanna sat again. "Ugh! Everyone thinks that. We...just knew it was time to move on, both of us."

Speculation crossed Ali's face, but he didn't ask if she'd slept with Jonathan. For that, she was eternally grateful. "And now, you have issues with Kristoff. What will you do if we cannot find our blackmailer in time?"

Good question. She'd been putting that decision off. This was her year to win; she couldn't imagine forfeiting. But... "If we don't succeed in fishing this blackmailer out, I won't have a choice. I like Kristoff. He's so talented. He's got great work ethic—"

"But you have no problem leaving him behind?"

"It's business."

"And you will not let anything or anyone stand in your way, will you?"

His soft question nearly crushed her with guilt. She shoved the feeling aside. Giving up over half her life and the chance to finally reach her dreams? "I can't.

7

*A*lejandro paced in the security room, watching the cameras positioned over *Sneak Peek's* front door. He checked his watch. Eight-forty five. People were beginning to stream in, in greater numbers than usual for this time of night on a Thursday.

The word about his scene with Shanna was out. He and Del had seen to it personally, not using names, of course...but socializing everywhere that it would be special.

The stage was set—if Shanna showed up. Now he worried she wouldn't. After all, the woman who prided herself on punctuality was fifteen minutes late. Was she trying to make a statement or yank his chain? Or was there some other reason she refused to come here tonight? What could possibly be more important to her than losing? Not embarrassment or modesty. She'd already survived her first public scene, which was always the most nerve-wracking. But one thing he had noticed? Every time he tried to get close to Shanna, she seemed increasingly anxious and tense.

Was it possible she feared being close to him more than she feared losing?

"You're wearing out the carpet," Del teased.

Ali shot him a dark glare. "She's not coming."

"She'll be here. You said yourself the woman is prickly and contrary for the purpose of being such. You admitted that she likes to control her situation, so it can't have been easy on her when you told her when to show up, what to wear...and nothing about what she could expect."

All of that was true, yet he'd had a larger purpose than being a controlling jackass. "I want Shanna to lean on me. I want her to know that she can trust me."

He wanted her to see what it felt like for someone to stand by her, even if she wasn't winning.

"You can't force her to figure that out."

"Normally, I would not try, but with Shanna..." He sighed and stared at the video cameras that showed no sign of her arrival. "If I cannot find some way now to encourage her to latch on to me, she will slip through my fingers."

Del shrugged. "Why does it matter? I mean, I agree she will be helpful in finding whoever has violated the club's rules, but we can flush out the asshole with or without her."

"She is not business to me; she's personal."

"How personal?"

Interpretation: how deep were his feelings? That question had been plaguing him all day. Shanna was more to him than catching a scumbag blackmailer, more than an amazing lay, more than an intriguing woman. Analyzing how it had happened and why was pointless. It was what it was, and Alejandro always trusted his gut.

"I think I am in love."

"That was fast. Less than a week." Del arched a dark brow.

"More time will not change what I feel, except to make it deeper. She is strong and vulnerable, smart, adorably stubborn, and in utter need of someone to love. How can I resist?" He flashed Del a self-deprecating smile.

"How, indeed? If you intend to resist, figure it out fast. She's here."

Ali whipped his gaze up to the bank of cameras and smiled.

"Aww. She's wearing a damn trench coat," Del groused.

Laughter bubbled up inside Alejandro. "Of course she is." Her little rebellion. "But I will bet she wore what I sent her underneath."

"I can't wait for this." Del rubbed his hands together.

With blood burning a path through his veins, Ali burst out of the security office and stalked toward the front door. Del followed close behind.

Alejandro intercepted Shanna two seconds after she walked in. "*Querida*, are you all right?"

As Shanna strode in, she lifted her lashes in a skittish glance. "Fine. Why wouldn't I be?"

Her guarded tone sent off alarm bells. So she was trying to push her armor back in place, put distance between them. He frowned. Perhaps he had pushed her too hard last night...or made her feel too guilty.

"When you did not arrive at eight-thirty, I grew concerned."

"No need."

He reached up to help her with her coat. She jerked away. "Don't. Just wait until..."

"We are on stage and I'm supposed to perform by fucking you?"

She swallowed and sent him a shaky nod that seared his guts with panic. After tonight, she was going to turn around and walk out of his life if he didn't think fast.

"Is something wrong?" He gentled his expression.

She looked away. "This is business. You're doing what you need to do. So am I."

"Shanna, this is not a business dealing or mere sex to me. I want it to be more than that for you, too."

She shot him a wary stare. "Until Saturday, I have to focus on fixing my problem. You want me to dance for the joy of it, not for the trophy. I can't be joyful if I already know before I dance a step that I can't win."

Alejandro sighed. He'd hoped he'd gotten through to her during their ice cream date, at least in some small way. But he'd been deluding himself. She was determined to shut him out and focus on nothing but the prize.

"Not to interrupt, kids," Del said, "but you need to make your way back to the room so you can get started. Showtime is in eight minutes."

Resisting the urge to rake a hand through his hair, Ali gnashed his teeth. He needed a minute to collect a few props and his thoughts.

"Can you show her to the room?" he asked his business partner. "I'll be there in five."

Ali didn't wait for the answer. He brushed past them, into the security corridor, and let the door slam behind him. Dread and anger crashed to the bottom of his stomach. Unless he acted fast, this could well be his last chance with Shanna. He had three minutes to figure out how to turn her head in his direction, convince her he wasn't simply out to save his business or get laid, and persuade her they could be more permanent partners beyond tonight.

Miracle, anyone?

～

*D*el escorted Shanna through the club. She was aware of people all around her swaying and writhing to the techno music. But her thoughts... Alejandro had the lock on those.

Last night and today, he'd acted like he cared. Why? She'd told him over and over this was business.

Yeah, did it feel like business when he was deep inside you, making you scream? Or when he fed you ice cream and did his best to be there for you?

The man had her so confused. What should have been nothing more than a temporary arrangement for the sake of ferreting out a mutual enemy—and okay, maybe a little mutual pleasure—had suddenly become very tangled. In the space of a few days, she'd come to think of Ali as a fixture in her life. The thought of that fixture being removed hurt.

So dangerous. How could she focus on the competition with everything hanging over her head if she had to add new and scary emotions for Alejandro to the mix?

"Follow me," Del said.

They crossed the dance floor and pushed aside a couple panting heatedly and letting their fingers do the walking. He escorted Shanna into a long hallway. At the end, he held a door open.

One peek inside, and she sucked in a surprised gasp. This was out of a fantasy! Plush, like a Pasha's palace. Rust, gold, bronze, with accents of black and cream. An enormous bed. Pillows everywhere.

The audience would be bigger in this room. And closer. The odds of someone to bringing in a camera was definitely greater.

"We've got the security angles covered," Del assured her before she even opened her mouth. "There are cameras all over this place. We've spent all day rigging it up. If someone tries to film you here, we'll nail him."

He wandered closer. Shanna tensed. Truth be told, the man made her nervous. He was dark like Alejandro. Both men had a wide streak of bad boy. Ali was like a fire, hot and sometimes unpredictable, never quite tamed. But Del...he could be a very cool customer. He'd do everything on his terms, in his time, his way. And show zero emotion doing it.

Now, he gave off the vibe of a predator. Shanna swallowed and raised her chin as he sauntered closer.

"Can I take your coat?"

Feeling too vulnerable for her comfort, she unbelted the garment and stripped it off. The red corset underneath and the matching black thong, garters, and stockings went way beyond suggestive. Being naked would make her feel more clothed.

Del whistled, looking her up and down, lingering on her breasts. "You look hot. Damn hot."

She cleared her throat. His hungry gaze eating her up when she'd last been on stage with Alejandro had turned her on. Being alone with him, having him this close, while he wore that ravenous expression? Disturbing.

She shrugged off his comment casually. "A costume like any other."

"You and Ali got a real thing going?"

Shanna frowned. When this was over, it was unlikely she and

Alejandro continue to see each other. They were from different worlds. Whatever they might have had would be another casualty to her ambition. It didn't bother her. Well...it shouldn't.

But something wretched and heavy that felt an awful lot like regret smothered her. Pain followed. It wouldn't do anything but distract her, so she shoved it down.

"No."

Flashing her a hot smile, Del leaned in until he was invading her personal space. "That's good news. Very good, in fact."

The rapacious way he watched her gave her major pause.

"When you and Ali are done here...maybe you and I could hook up?" he dragged a fingertip down her arm, leaving a prickle of unease in his wake.

Did Del really imagine that after having sex with his friend and business partner, she was just going to throw Ali over and hop in his bed?

She put space between them. "I don't think so. Get your hand off me."

He complied slowly. "If you and Ali don't have a thing going, why not? You're a gorgeous woman. I've seen you in action, and you make me hard. I'll treat you right, make you scream. I hear you're good at switching partners. C'mon. What do you say?"

He reached around her and slung his hand low on her hip, almost on her ass.

Fury erupted in Shanna's gut. She grabbed his wrist, squeezed his pressure point until he winced, then shoved his hand away from her backside.

"What the hell are you thinking? No, the better question is, which part of your body is doing the thinking for you? I'm pretty sure I know the answer." She cut a derisive glare in the vicinity of his crotch, then shot a quick glance to the door. Where was Ali?

"What's the problem, baby?" He moved in closer again.

Her temper flared. *Douche bag!*

She lifted her foot and dug her stiletto into his toes. He swore, and she smiled. "The problem is, I'm supposed to have sex with your friend in less than five minutes. Let's focus, shall we?"

His voice was strained as he reached down to cradle his injured toe. "You don't get sentimental about your partners. And you said you weren't involved with Ali. So why shouldn't I ask a gorgeous woman if she wants to hook up?"

Why, indeed? Del was attractive physically. She doubted he would be demanding of her time or try to delve into her psyche. Del would never take her to his bed after a wild night on stage, love her privately, and rip past the barriers around her heart. He would probably never press her for more than sex.

But if she disliked Alejandro for all those things, why wasn't she eager to spend alone time with his sinfully good-looking friend?

"Alejandro is your business partner and best friend."

"Yeah, but if you're not into him, that makes you fair game."

Shanna was still processing Del's words when he grabbed her and crushed her body against his. His mouth swooped down, and he captured her lips. At the first swipe of his tongue against hers, she knew nothing but panic.

And pure rage.

She twisted in his grasp until she delivered a hard knee to his balls. He backed away instantly, doubled over and clutching himself.

"What the hell is your problem?"

"I'll tell you exactly what I've told Alejandro: I have the most important competition of my career to focus on. I intend to win, and anything else is just a distraction I don't need."

"And that's your only reason for turning me down?"

~

*A*lejandro shoved the stage door open. It collided with the wall, echoing across the stage as he strode inside. He had the distinct impression he'd interrupted something.

In the middle, Shanna stood wearing the corset, garters, and thong he'd sent her—and looking every bit as drop-dead sexy as he'd known she would. Though his dick was already hard at the thought of being inside her, this outfit added to the red blood cell count below his waist.

But the righteous anger on her face made him pause. Especially when he saw Del two feet away, hunched over, clutching his balls and glaring at her.

What the hell?

"She's got a mean knee, man."

"He's got the disposition of a manwhore."

Anger crashed into Alejandro with the same impact as driving a hundred miles an hour straight into a brick wall. "You made a move on her?"

"Yes!" Shanna shouted.

Del tried to stand up straight and shrug. "You said she had a habit of switching dance partners. I wondered if that extended to sex. She swore you two had nothing going. If that's true, why would she kick me?"

Then his friend did something bizarre. He winked.

Ali frowned...until everything started falling into place. Del had been testing her. If Shanna didn't care a thing about him, Alejandro knew she would have gone for Del. Women did—in droves. Shanna had been turned on by him watching her just days ago. Why not follow through?

Ali suspected that the only reason Shanna had kneed his pal was because whatever feelings she had developed between them since their last scene together were stronger than she wanted to admit. And Del had pissed her off.

Suddenly, Ali resisted the urge to smile. Hope curled in his belly, warmed his heart, made his dick even stiffer. He'd test his theory tonight.

"We have no time to argue. Let us start this party. Del, show the crowd in. Security tells me they are lined up down the hallway. Shanna, turn around and put your hands behind your back."

With a nod, Del turned and headed for the door.

No surprise, Shanna hesitated at his command. She'd assumed

he would be angry that Del made a pass at her. She'd assumed Ali would behave possessively. If he hadn't known Del for years and hadn't known quite well how his friend's mind worked, Ali would have been.

Instead, he intended to enjoy the fireworks between he and Shanna before he got to the bottom of whatever was in her heart. Del was just helping him along.

"Is there a problem?" he asked. "People will begin filing in soon. We should be in position."

"Fine." She presented him with her back.

What a luscious view! Feminine shoulders tapered down to a narrow, red-corseted back. The black thong bisected a firm, feminine ass he'd fantasized about fucking. Those garters and black thigh-high stockings hugging the toned curves of her legs damn near had him on his knees.

And if he played his cards right, she would be all his.

Forcing his stare back to her wrists crossed at the small of her back, Ali grabbed them. With a flick and two quick clicks, he secured her in handcuffs.

She whirled on him, murder in her eyes. "What the hell are you doing? Unlatch these! I didn't sign up for this. We didn't discuss—"

Ali cut off her tirade by cupping her nape and covering her mouth with his. She struggled...for a moment. Then he swept inside her mouth, tunneled his hands in her hair, and kissed her as if his very life depended on it.

She melted.

With a gentle nip and a soothing kiss to cover the sting, he pulled back and whispered, "We have an audience."

Releasing her, Ali walked a half circle around her and cozied up to her back, letting her feel the heat of his body and his erection. She gasped.

The curve of her neck beckoned, and he trailed his lips up the graceful line and soft skin.

Briefly, he opened his eyes and discovered at least twenty-five people in the room—and more filing in. Perfect. Maybe they would catch the asshole tonight.

Then he put everything out of his mind—except Shanna.

He started at her shoulders, but his hands seemed to develop a mind of their own. Down they plunged, right over the curves of her breasts, pushed up by the tight corset. But having those nipples covered wasn't going to do.

In a few seconds, Alejandro brushed through the little fastenings holding the garment together. It fell to the stage in a boned rustle of fabric.

Men groaned in the audience as he bared her breasts to them. Shanna tensed. Ali could feel her shivering. Cold? He didn't think so. Nerves? Maybe. Excitement. Definitely. He could smell a hint of her arousal.

Eagerly, he reached around and cupped her breasts in his hands, squeezing her nipples between his thumbs and fingers. She writhed, wriggling her ass against his cock.

He was about to lose his mind.

With a yank, he tugged the sheer thong from her body. Another collective groan rang from the audience. Guys shifted weight from one foot to another, adjusted themselves in their pants, sat forward in their chairs. Shanna began to pant.

Ali dragged his palms down her abdomen. He itched to feel the silk of her pussy, see just how wet she was.

Moments later, he had his answer. She was wet, welcoming, lush. Shanna might lie about her feelings for him, but her body couldn't.

Now was the perfect time to start testing his theory...

A quick point at Del brought his friend up on the stage. Shanna tensed again. This time, he didn't think it was due to excitement.

Before she could say a word, he whispered, "I want to watch your breasts be sucked. Del will help us out."

"No," she whimpered.

"You change partners all the time. Why does it matter?"

Del approached her and pressed his body close to Shanna's. Ali didn't say a word, just lifted her breasts up to him.

Just before he bent to her, Del sent her a smile that said he was ready for scorching hot sex.

"It just matters," she whispered. "Please no."

Lifting dark eyes to Ali, Del waited for a cue.

Ali had what he wanted for now. He shook his head.

With a wry grin, Del contented himself by placing a chaste kiss on the curve of her breast. But to show he wasn't going to be dismissed, he took a seat on a nearby pillow and sent a scorching stare her way.

In truth, Ali knew they had to play along, just in case their blackmailer was in the room. But he wanted nothing more than to get Shanna alone. *Soon*, he promised himself.

Turning her back toward him, Ali watched her stage smile collapse. She looked at him with a mixture of hurt, anger, and relief. Apparently, swapping partners did matter to her. And he sensed that the sooner he got her to admit that about dance, the sooner she'd settle into having one man in her life.

Impatient to touch her, Ali tore down the zipper of his leather pants and freed his stiff cock. "Suck me."

He kicked a pillow under her knees. Shanna hesitated, then sank down, bent her head, and consumed him.

Oh, hell. Her mouth was a silken oven, soft and scorching and robbing him of breath. She damn sure knew what to do with that tongue of hers, caressing the length of his staff, curling it around the head. She sucked deep and hard, all the way to the back of her throat.

His heartbeat rattled in his chest. His ears buzzed with the excitement. Faintly, he was aware of male groans and a "fuck, yeah," from the audience. But focusing beyond Shanna's hot mouth was growing impossible.

As wonderful as it was, it had to stop. They had a show to put on for these guests—and a potential blackmailer. A blow job was all well and good, but not blackmail-worthy, compared to Kristoff's show.

With a groan of regret, Ali cupped her cheeks and lifted her mouth from his cock. Then he helped her to her feet. In four steps, he had her bent over the huge, cushioned bed, her breasts pressed to the silk comforter. A few seconds later, he was sheathed and deep inside her.

She gripped him like no one ever had, like every contour had been formed just to clench around him perfectly.

He seized her hips and tunneled deeper. Then set a ruthless pace.

She cried out. The sight of her all spread out under him, her hands still cuffed at the small of her back, her pussy taking every inch he had...hell, he wasn't going to last long. And he didn't want to go off alone.

"I ache to play with your clit and feel you orgasm around me..." He hadn't even finished the sentence before he slid a pair of determined fingers right over the button of her nerves.

With his other hand, he gripped her hips tight. He thrust inside her repeatedly, dragging the head of his cock right over that sensitive spot that had her muscles tensing, shaking.

In moments, a low, feminine groan split the air. Almost there...

"Come for me," he demanded. "Come!"

With another brush and press of his fingers over her clit, she screamed. Around them, the audience groaned. Several stroked their own cocks...even Del.

Then the rippling walls of her sex contracted, tightened, gripping and coaxing him, blotting out all other thoughts. Ali closed his eyes and focused on her. He shouted through clenched teeth as he followed her into ecstasy.

More than one groan of satisfaction split the air within moments. Ali didn't care. All he knew was that underneath him was the woman he would not let go of. They had seen to business.

Now it was time for the real pleasure—and hopefully, the future —to begin.

a pleasure cloud. Heavy limbs, light head. A gentle throb between her legs pulsing as it slowly abated. Alejandro's embrace providing warmth, even as he gripped her as if he'd never let go. Ah...

Shanna could happily stay here, connected to him for a while. A long while. There were reasons she shouldn't, she knew. She just couldn't remember them now.

Then Alejandro slipped free of her body and broke her sensual haze. She lifted weighty lids to watch him walk past her and snap the curtains shut between them and the audience. Del remained on their side of the drape, and Shanna was suddenly conscious of her nudity and Del's dark eyes on her.

"Keep them the hell out of here," Alejandro growled in low tones.

Del clapped his gaze on his buddy, who was now buttoning his pants and wearing a sly smile. "You got it. Tomorrow?"

Ali smiled. "Maybe the day after."

What were they talking about? It should be obvious, but her brain was so clouded by satisfaction that thinking was just a lot of effort right now.

Del's laugh barely registered when Alejandro turned and stalked across the floor to her. In seconds, he uncuffed one of her wrists, grabbed her up in his arms, and headed for the stage door.

"What...? Where are you—?"

"Alone." He said the word like a vow. "No one except you and me, being us together."

Just in case others could hear, she whispered, "But the blackmailer—"

"If he was here tonight, he already got what he came for. Del will call me if they captured something on the security cameras. Now, this is about us."

"But you said we would stay all night, if necessary."

He stopped. "Is that what you want, for me to fuck you again for an audience? Shall we invite more people in this time?"

Sarcasm. Anger. And she understood. Something inside her rejected the notion of more audience time, too. "No."

"Good. I'm done sharing you with other hungry male eyes." He pushed through a door, out into a bright hall, past the open door to security. Laughing and clapping ensued from the crew inside the office, and Shanna buried her head in his neck.

"I'm naked!" she shrieked.

"They just watched us on the cameras. They are not seeing anything they have not yet seen. Which is another reason I want you all to myself."

Shanna didn't have the chance to speak again before Ali opened another door and let it slam behind him. Now it was dark, and Southern California's summer evening sky simmered all around them in a velvet hush. Frogs and crickets hummed in the sultry breeze. The lights of the city beyond the hill twinkled and winked as far as she could see.

"It's beautiful out here."

"That I would rather look at you should tell you how I feel about *your* beauty."

Shanna snapped her gaze up to Ali's. No smile. His stare was full of gravity—and rising need.

"Alejandro, maybe we should talk about—"

"No. Tonight is about you and me. No conversation, no people, no blackmail, no cameras. I need to feel you like I have never needed before."

She gaped, totally unable to deny the breathless rush of joy at his words. Did he...care about her?

There was no time to ponder the answer before he spirited her into his cottage, through the intimate cocoon of the hushed night, straight to his bed. In the shadows, she could make out its straight lines and modern flare. It was big, dark, exotic—just like the man.

Then his mattress was at her back, and he grabbed the empty cuff dangling from her wrist, and Shanna expected him to attach it to his bed somehow so he would have her at his mercy.

Instead, he attached the cuff to his own wrist.

They were joined. Together. Bound.

"Alejandro?"

He didn't answer. Instead, he tossed the handcuff key somewhere on the floor, far out of reach, then covered her mouth with his own.

Shanna expected his ravenous hunger, a hard-edged *boom-fast-now* kind of touch. She was shocked instead by his soft insistence. His kiss was seduction itself. Thorough, unhurried. Slow, deep. Unabashedly intimate, as he conveyed his every want, spoke with his soul, communicating only using his mouth.

It was impossible not to fall under his spell.

A new ribbon of desire tied her stomach in knots as he trailed hot kisses across her cheek, down toward her neck. He exhaled against her neck, close to her ear, stirring sensitive skin. She shivered as his lips caressed her, branded her. He swept a fingertip down the arch of her throat and nipped at her lobe.

"Necesito tocarle, su cara, su piel. Su corazón."

Shanna had no idea what his words meant, but they melted her. In that moment, whatever he wanted, she wanted, too.

"Tell me..."

He didn't right away. Instead, he swept his mouth over hers again. The tangle of breaths, lips, tongues became a deliberate kiss of endless hunger. Eloquent, shockingly sexual as the fingers of his free hand sifted into her hair, curling possessively around the strands. Sizzlingly intimate as he tore his mouth from hers to stare, penetrating her with eyes like burning coals in the pitch of night. Ensnared, Shanna could not look away.

"I said that I need to touch you, your face, your skin. Your heart."

Something both shocked and joyous burst inside her. She gasped, and Alejandro swallowed the sound with another drugging kiss.

With every brush of his lips, every glide of his hot palm, every male moan poured into her mouth he ripped past her barriers until she opened completely to him—parting her lips wider to accept more of his possession, clutching one hard shoulder with her free hand to keep him near, spreading her thighs to invite him inside. She sighed when his narrow hips fit right into the curve of her body as if he'd been made to fill her.

"Yes." She arched under him, unable to hold anything back.

He nestled his free hand under the curve in her back, keeping her breasts and the damp heat of her skin right against him.

"Yo le tocaré toda la noche. Cada parte de tú sabrás el se siente de mí."

"Ali...please."

The way he touched her, as if he had not another thought in his head except pleasing her... She burned inside her skin, yet she knew only he could save her. He would shatter her into a million pieces first, then remake her into a new woman. A warning bell went off in some distant part of her mind, but his fingers gripped her hips, fitting her directly against the hard column of his erection. He wound down her body and brushed soft lips against the side of her breast.

"I *will* touch you all night long," he translated. "Every part of you will know the feel of me."

She had no doubt Alejandro would keep that promise.

He suckled her nipples over and over, lavishing attention on her until they stood red, swollen, so sensitive that nothing more than his breath on her induced a shiver. All the while, his fingers free from the cuff whispered across her skin. Her back, her thighs, her buttocks. Even her knees, calves, and toes. Alejandro put that hand on every inch of available skin, finally drawing her leg up high on his hip so he could toy with the sensitive underside of her knee.

Gently, he rode her clit with his erection. Not pushing or grinding. Not bruising. Instead, a soft nudge of delicious pressure in a hypnotic rhythm, one that took her higher and higher.

The seed of pleasure under her clit sprouted and bloomed. Shanna panted, trying to resist the searing pleasure for just another moment. She dug the fingers not bound by the cuff into the hard flesh of his back, pressing down his body, far down, until she gripped his ass in her hand.

Moonlight spilled past the open blinds, swirling in on the evening breeze as he whispered, "*La piel estas rosácea, mi amor. Eres maduro y listo, sí?*"

"Tell me, Ali!" She moaned. "Please..."

"Your skin is rosy, my love. You are ripe and ready, yes?"

"Yes. Yes, now!"

He pressed against her again, nudging her clit with his cock. The cream of her arousal spread all over his flesh, and the next time he rocked against her, the bead of nerves he teased leaped at the slick pressure. Blood rushed south, pooled between her legs, gathering need, pleasure, and anticipation right where it impacted her most. She clawed, cried in his arms.

"Who is here, Shanna? Who is in this room?"

"Us. Just us."

"*Apenas tú y mí. Ninguna audiencia. Ninguna cámaras. Nosotros.*" He breathed as he gathered the crooks of her knees into his arms. "Just you and me. No audience, no cameras. *Us.*"

The way it always should be. The thought ran through Shanna's mind unchecked, unchallenged, unstoppable as Alejandro paused, probed, then on a long glide, he penetrated her.

His hard flesh filled her sex, sank deep, deeper, then deeper still. Making love face to face...totally different than being dominated by him for an audience. The slick rasp of his engorged shaft raked against her sensitive walls. A jolt of pleasure coiled, tightened, intensifying, growing faster than she could assimilate.

"So tight, my love," he murmured as he drew back and brought their cuffed hands up to her breast. Her palm cupped her flesh as his thumb caressed her nipple. It was as if they were seeing to her pleasure together, and it drove Shanna mad with delirious need.

All the while, the slow steady pleasure of his thrusts made her into a wild woman. She writhed, lifted her hips, arched—anything to reach more of him, lure him deeper still into her.

Alejandro went willingly, every lingering slide of his erection inside her lifting her arousal higher. Her pulse pounded in her ears. Heat suffused her body. She could barely breathe. And she didn't care.

For the first time in years—maybe in her life—she didn't just feel; she was wholly alive, driven by something more than a statue of faux gold molded like dancers she wanted to someday sit on her mantle. She lived for now. She lived to feel the man growling words in a language she didn't understand but adored as he strained to fulfill every promise of pleasure boiling in her body.

Alejandro gripped the hand joined to his by the cuff and laced their fingers together. He squeezed her hand tight as their breaths merged, their cries mingled. "Come for me."

The request from his mouth became a demand from his body as he thrust straight into her core again.

Shanna splintered into a million pieces, blinded by the brilliant pleasure bursting inside her. In the next moment, he followed her into the white-hot rush of shattering pleasure. Oh, god. He was all over her, everywhere...inside her. Shanna doubted she could wash his possession away with a mere shower. It seemed unlikely that time and distance would completely free her from him.

She feared she'd given a piece of herself to Alejandro she'd likely never get back: her heart.

～

*S*ated and exhausted, Shanna pulled up in the driveway of the house she'd been raised in. She and all of her siblings had moved out years ago. Dad had stayed in the rambling house alone. Why, she didn't know. The place was haunted by the ghost of her mother, a woman she vaguely remembered smiling and dancing around the kitchen.

She should have gone home first. Showered, changed, had a cup of coffee before coming here. If she had stayed in Ali's bed, he would have offered her all that and more. Instead, she'd pleaded the need to use the bathroom and persuaded him to unlock the cuffs joining them. She'd waited a few minutes, until she was sure he'd drifted back to sleep, then dressed in one of his shirts and a pair of long sweatpants, then sneaked out. Not that it mattered. Ali was with her, in her, in a way that had nothing to do with the fact they'd had unprotected sex and everything to do with the fact she cared far more about him than she should.

The chilly California air of the early morning hadn't helped to sort out her head. She was in love with a man who would never mean to stand in the way of her dance dreams, but how could Alejandro not, as consuming as he was? She'd barely driven two miles from *Sneak Peek*, and she'd begun to feel the withdrawal of his warmth, his acceptance and tenderness.

Dangerous. She was the Bitch of the Ballroom because she'd adhered to strict discipline and a ruthless dedication to perfection. She intended to win that long-coveted trophy, damn it. When the music was high and the lights down low, the judges didn't care what was deep in her heart. She'd do well to remember that.

Still, those moments in Ali's arms... For the first time in years, maybe ever, she'd felt adored, and not because of what she might achieve or what competition she might win. She didn't have anything to prove in that moment. Alejandro cared about her. He proved that in amazing, pleasure-drenched ways every time he touched her.

Now, she clutched a bag of bagels and cream cheese, along with a portable carafe of coffee she'd purchased at a bakery, and let herself into the house.

Shanna followed the smell of burned toast with a poignant smile.

She sauntered into the kitchen and looked at her father, older now, gray at the temples, his reading glasses askew, but still vital and well built for pushing sixty.

"Bagels?" she offered.

Her dad plucked charred bread from the toaster with his fingertips, then dropped it on the counter with a curse.

Then he skewered her with a stare. "Sure. As soon as you explain why you're wearing men's clothes, are rosy with whisker burn, and smell like sex."

Certainly nothing off about his eyesight.

"I do things beyond work and practice at the dance studio."

He sent her a pointed stare over the top of his glasses. "I never noticed it until today. You've always been very single-minded about winning."

"I still am. What happened last night won't happen again." She passed him the bag of bagels, hoping it would distract him.

He ignored the gesture and arched a sharp brow, as if he disapproved. But Shanna couldn't shake the impression that he was suppressing a smile.

"I suspected it would happen someday. Maybe it's the female way. Who is he?"

Shanna frowned. "What do you mean, 'the female way?'"

He shrugged. "Women follow their hearts, which usually lead them to some man or another, who may or may not respect their desire to keep pursuing their goals."

Exactly. No doubt, he'd have complete disrespect if she ultimately made that choice. Her brothers, too.

"Which is precisely why Alejandro and I are...done."

"Alejandro? Do I know him?"

Shanna shook her head. "Argentinean. He owns a nightclub. We met at the benefit for the Catholic orphans charity last weekend."

God, it was weird to be discussing her love life with her father in the kitchen of her childhood home at seven in the morning. She needed coffee for this.

"Hmm." Her father hesitated. "What does he think of your dancing?"

"I assume he's okay with it. Not that it matters." Shanna sipped the caffeine-laden brew and let it sink into her hazy brain.

He reached for the carafe of coffee and poured a steaming mug. "A hindrance, is he? Resenting your practices?"

"No." Not unless she was avoiding him.

"Latin men are notoriously jealous. He can't handle your time with Kristoff and the way your partner has to touch you?"

Shanna had to laugh. "No, he knows way too much about Kristoff to be jealous."

"So you're just worried he'd be a general distraction?"

"He would. The other night, I was headed for a sensible dinner and an early evening to bed. Big day of practice the next morning, which is vital with the competition coming up. He came by and just assumed I'd go out for ice cream with him."

"Ice cream. That's a huge problem." Her father sipped his coffee, seemingly deep in thought.

Somehow, Shanna got the impression he was laughing silently at her.

"It is! I can't afford to blow off sleep and eat a gallon of ice cream to satisfy some romantic notion of his. And then he tells me personal stuff, about his childhood and friendships. He blurts out his views that commitment is absolute and infidelity is inexcusable. Why tell *me*? The whole incident is taking up my thoughts that should be directed to the competition, which is tomorrow. And last night, he kept me up half the night..."

Realizing she'd nearly spilled the details of her sex life, Shanna flushed, then continued with a safer topic. "The man is just consuming. Him just *being* steals my attention and leads my thoughts astray. Every trick I've used in the past to ward off would-be Romeos doesn't work with him. He just doesn't give up and won't go away."

"And you're so tempted to let him into your life that it frightens you." It wasn't a question. He seemed to *know* that's exactly how she felt.

"How...?" She grappled to find the right words. "You know?"

"Your mother had a life before we married. Did you know she was a prima ballerina?"

A prima ballerina? No clue. "I knew she flitted around the kitchen and she was graceful..."

But her mother had died years ago. In some ways, her mother was as great a mystery to her as she would be if Shanna had never met her.

"American Ballet Theater. She was set to star in the season's *Giselle*. To this day, I'll never know what she saw in a cocky weightlifter coming fresh off a gold medal high. I had to have been a complete ass. But she claimed to love me. God knows the sun rose and set on that woman, as far as I was concerned."

Shanna frowned, sensing that she would not like what came next.

"You married her and—"

"Encouraged her to stop dancing. Made sure I got her pregnant with your brother so she had to stay beside me. I was a hugely selfish bastard where her time and energy were concerned. If I could take it back somehow and let her take her rightful place on stage..."

Mouth gaping open, Shanna stared at her father. *This* was the man who had driven her for years. Nothing she'd ever done was ever good enough. Second place was first loser. Quitting was the professional equivalent of a noose.

"I don't understand."

"I know." He sighed heavily and sat on one of the little wooden chairs they'd had forever. "I pushed you and pushed you. I don't think I realized until just now that I did it because I wanted to make up for what I did to your mother. She never said that she regretted her decision. But I'd catch her every so often holding her toe shoes with a wistful look on her face. I suspect she always wondered what could have been. I didn't want you wondering, too."

Shanna gaped, shock ricocheting through her. Her father had intentionally killed her mother's dance dream? And regretted it like hell. For years, he'd driven Shanna, fueled her ambition. As a child, she'd wanted to follow one of her brothers into their sports, but he'd specifically signed her up for dance class after dance class. Now she knew why. But...

"You sound as if you're encouraging me to continue with Alejandro. Why change your mind now?"

He stirred his cooling coffee. "In retrospect, I don't think your mother really regretted her decision to leave dance and marry. After she was gone, I realized how short her life had been cut and that I'd prevented her from fulfilling her dream. I regretted standing in her way. I beat myself up a lot over it. But you know, most of my memories are of her smiling. Your mother used to have this one little grin when she was particularly happy. A little lopsided, with a dimple in her left cheek and a twinkle in her eye. When I think about that smile now, I know she was at peace with her life." Her father paused, looked up at her. "Until this morning, I'd never seen that smile on you. But there was a moment when you got out of your car. I was watching through the window. I saw that smile on your face. I'm guessing Alejandro put it there."

He had. When she pushed aside her tumult about tomorrow's competition, happiness sneaked in, again and again. The thought that, after last night, she might never see Alejandro again, gouged her with deep shards of pain. And it shouldn't. Their relationship had been short. Intense, yes, but nothing to build a lifetime on?

Why did she feel like she was selling them short?

"He sounds like the kind of guy who wouldn't demand you give up your dream," her father said. "If he can make you happy and give you the freedom to pursue what you want professionally, why aren't you grabbing onto him with both hands?"

Yeah, why not? "With him as a distraction, I may never win."

"Would you rather lose a competition or the man you love?"

"It's not that simple, Dad. If I...divide my time, I won't be as dedicated. If I never become a champion, you won't think I'm weak?"

"Would it really matter if I did?"

Shanna paused. Thought. Alejandro's love or her dad's approval?

No choice. "It would bother me if you weren't proud, but I'm an adult." She drew in a deep breath as her realization became an admission. "I should be doing what makes me happy."

"Yes, and you need a man's love more than Daddy's blessing."

She nodded. "Jason, Ash, and Kyle would make fun of me if I chose to be with Alejandro."

Her dad rolled his eyes. "They'd make fun of you no matter what you did. They're convinced that's their prerogative as big brothers."

In spite of the weirdness of the conversation, Shanna laughed. "You think?"

The smile faded as something occurred to her. "I'm not sure matters with Alejandro will be as simple as me expressing my feelings. Let's say I've played very hard to get. He may not be talking to me after I, um...sneaked out on him this morning."

"Why don't you send him tickets to tomorrow's competition? I bet he shows. I want to meet the man who managed to see beyond your Bitch of the Ballroom act."

"You're coming tomorrow?"

He reached across the table and squeezed her hand. "I wouldn't miss it for the world. Whether you're crowned champion of the ballroom or of Alejandro's heart, I'm proud no matter what."

9

*W*aiting in the darkened corner of the ballroom's dance floor, Shanna drew in a deep breath, smoothed her hair, straightened her sleeve, shifted her weight. And scanned the crowd—again.

Nothing.

"You must not fidget."

If she hadn't been so nervous, she would have laughed at Kristoff. Why not just tell her she shouldn't breathe? "I know. Sorry."

"You are nervous?" her big, blond partner stood behind her and whispered in her ear. "Do you fear losing?"

The competition? Not as much as she thought. They would lose, of course, and during her largely sleepless night, she'd come to accept that. Kristoff had only been living his personal life, and he'd tried to engage in his kink of choice in a responsible environment. It wasn't his fault someone had it out for her and had circumvented *Sneak Peek's* rules to hurt her. But Alejandro? She absolutely feared losing him. In fact, she suspected she already had.

Shanna had delivered the tickets to *Sneak Peak* in person this morning. Del had greeted her at the door. Actually, greeted was a strong word. Met was more accurate. Reluctantly, in fact. His behavior had been considerably cooler than their last meeting. When he said he'd give the tickets to Ali, she added that she hoped he would visit her before the show so they could talk. Del had merely given her a terse nod, then shut the door in her face.

Clearly, she'd hurt Ali enough to seriously piss off Del.

Alejandro hadn't come to see her before the competition. Another scan of the ballroom...there sat her father, who waved. She smiled back, but she still didn't see Alejandro's coffee-dark hair, swagger, or sin-laced smile.

Had she pushed him away one too many times? The painful thought tightened her stomach into impossible knots. Throwing up didn't feel out of the question.

"Shanna, you are nervous about the routine?"

No. She and Kristoff were ready. Beyond ready. They knew these dances. They had perfected their chemistry and rhythm on the floor. The blackmailer's footage would keep them from winning, but they would give their best showing. She couldn't ask for more than that.

"Or do you regret that you were unable to replace me with a new partner in time for this competition?"

Scowling at his bitter tone, Shanna glanced over her shoulder at Kristoff. Mouth pinched, eyes tight, shoulders stiff. Damn, he looked nervous. Petrified. What was that about? He was never wound up before a competition. Maybe he was rattled about the video potentially circulating the judges' table? After all, this threat affected his career, too.

As Kristoff continued to watch her with narrow, burning eyes, and she replayed his question in her head, Shanna finally understood.

"I'm not replacing you." She dropped her arm to her side and reached for his hand. She gave it a friendly squeeze. "I never auditioned anyone else. You were right about the partner swapping; it was stupid."

He shot her a suspicious stare. "Why the change?"

"I used to bury my guilt about dropping someone for the sake of

winning. It never worked. You made me see how pointless it was."
With a little help from Ali and Del.

"You do not seek to replace me? Truly?"

She smiled. "You're stuck with me."

Kristoff leveled his mega-watt smile at her. "For days now, I
cannot stop from worrying you plan to replace me." He squeezed her
hand. "Thank you. I am happy now."

"We win or lose together, okay? Besides, maybe we haven't been
winning because we've forgotten that dancing isn't all serious.
Maybe...we just need to have fun with it tonight, see what
happens."

Kristoff hesitated, then teased, "Who are you and what have you
done with my partner?"

Despite her nerves and her worries about losing Ali, Shanna had
to laugh. If nothing else, she'd cemented one important relationship
tonight. And damn if it didn't feel good.

"If we were alone, I'd slug you for that."

"There is the Shanna I know and adore," Kristoff muttered.

Just then, the music ended, and the announcer reminded the
crowd of their competitors' names and number. Shanna drew in a
relaxing breath. *In. Out.* They were next.

"Before we go on, I must tell you something."

"Kristoff, we're about to be announced."

"This is true, but—"

"Couple number one hundred three, Shanna York and Kristoff
Palavin from Los Angeles, California."

The crowd's cheer wasn't as enthusiastic as Kristoff would like,
Shanna knew. She should care, she supposed, but right now, she
couldn't get past the fact that Alejandro had chosen not to use the
tickets she'd left him.

Which meant he'd given up on her, she feared for good.

Forcing a smile as the onlookers clapped, she walked onto the
dance floor, Kristoff beside her, cradling her palm in his. They struck
their pose and waited.

Doing her best to focus on the next three minutes, Shanna plastered on a smile and projected it to the crowd. The music burst over the quiet, Shanna arched, kicked, and turned.

There sat Alejandro.

His face gave away nothing, but the grin that shaped her mouth was her first real one of the day.

He's here. Here!

And he looked incredible in a black suit, white shirt, and a satiny charcoal tie.

She knew he looked even better out of the suit.

Before she whirled around to face Kristoff again, she flashed Ali a look she hoped communicated just how thrilled she was that he'd come.

Over the next two minutes, forty seconds, she and Kristoff poured their souls into the dance. And he was spectacular, as if some light had been turned on inside him. Relaxed yet crisp. Strong. God, he played to the crowd. He really was incredible. Shanna responded, acting the part of the seductive female to his commanding male in the cha-cha-cha.

No doubt in her mind, they sparkled, shined, brought the WOW to the dance floor. Shanna couldn't remember the last time she'd enjoyed dancing so much.

When the music ended, she knew they had done their best. Yes, she'd love to win tonight, but if it wasn't in the cards, they would spend a year living down the scandal and practicing their butts off. They would conquer this trophy next season.

The crowd stood, cheered, their enthusiasm catching. Never before had she felt so liked by the crowd, so connected to them as she and Kristoff bowed.

She turned her head slightly to see Alejandro. He, too, stood and clapped, then bent to whisper into the ear of a small but striking middle-aged woman who shared his eyes. His mother.

Then he turned his attention back to her, fixing burning hazel eyes on her, and Shanna felt the zing and sizzle all the way to her toes.

Damn, she loved that man.

"You and Alejandro?" Kristoff asked as they left the dance floor. "You have a...thing?"

"What?"

"You looked at him as if you cannot wait to devour him, as if you are all his. Or as if he is all yours. Is that true?"

Shanna swallowed a lump of nerves. God, she hoped Alejandro being here meant that he'd forgiven her for running away and being afraid to believe in them... If not, she wasn't giving up. No more switching partners for her when things got difficult—not professionally or personally.

"That's my plan."

⤳

"In fourth place..." the announcer droned, and Shanna listened long enough to realize her name hadn't been announced, then clapped politely.

This was usually the part of the event that made her most nervous. How many times had she stood at the corner of the stage, trying not to pass out, praying she would not be disappointed by failing to grab the trophy again, only to hear her name announced long before the first place winner's? How many times had she trotted out her plastic smile, like third place thrilled her, while feeling crushed inside? Too many.

But tonight...she almost *wanted* the announcer to call her name now, so she could finish this dog and pony show and talk to Alejandro. His face still gave away absolutely nothing, not anger, not joy. Had he forgiven her and come to be with her? Or had he simply come because she'd given him free tickets and his mother liked to attend? No clue. That man could probably play a mean game of poker.

"In third place..."

Again, not her name. Another polite clap. Another clandestine glance at Alejandro. He raised a brow at her, but his expression remained utterly, frustratingly unreadable. Forget the contest results. Not knowing how Ali felt about her was killing her.

And what did that say about how much she loved him? She was well and truly hooked.

"In second place..."

Not her name again. The couple beside them swept out on the floor, and Shanna could see the woman's forced smile hiding disappointment and the crushing blow of defeat.

But wait...if second place had been announced, and there were no other couples out on the floor...

"In first place, the California Dance Star Latin dance ballroom champions, couple one hundred three, Shanna York and Kristoff Palavin of Los Angeles!"

Kristoff squeezed her hand as he led her out onto the floor. "We did it! We did it!"

They had. Finally! Alejandro was clapping for her. His mother, too. The whole crowd, including her father, who enthusiastically whistled like he was at a football game. It was bad form in ballroom, but she smiled, glowed, and grinned from ear to ear.

Tonight, she was finally a champion.

But how had it happened, given the blackmailer's threats?

"What about...you know?" she said to Kristoff through her smile. Maybe the threatening bastard hadn't followed through?

Before he could answer, the emcee came forward with their trophy. Kristoff grabbed it with one hand and hoisted it up in the air, along with their joined hands. Together, they bowed.

Professionally, she had never been happier than in that moment.

"Ms. York and Mr. Palavin are now eligible to compete in the upcoming World Cup Latin competition."

Wow, a huge dream come true. And yet... Her life would be incomplete, her triumph hollow, if she didn't have Alejandro to share it with.

The emcee took the trophy from Kristoff. The lights dimmed, and as champions, she and Kristoff danced. But her mind was on Ali, the way he watched her, his face shuttered but his posture relaxed. What was the man thinking?

Soon, others crowded onto the floor. With the spotlight no longer on them, Shanna all but forced Kristoff to tango Alejandro's way.

Kristoff resisted. "I must tell you something."

"Later. Okay?"

"But—"

"Give me fifteen minutes."

Before he could reply, they reached the edge of the dance floor. She turned to Alejandro's mother.

"Mrs. Diaz? Hi, I'm Shanna York." She held out her hand.

"*Ella es su novia?*" his mother asked Ali sharply.

"*Mamá...*" He sighed. "*Sí.*" Then he whispered something in her ear...and her entire face changed, lightened, glowed.

She turned to Shanna with a beaming smile and said in accented English. "Thank you for the tickets. Congratulations on winning, *nuera.*"

Nuera? Damn she was going to have to learn to speak Spanish at the first opportunity. "Thank you. Have you had the pleasure of dancing with my partner, Kristoff?"

She shook her head and risked a shy peek at Kristoff. "He is one of my favorites."

"I'm sure he'd consider it a favor. He gets tired of dancing with me and would love your company." Shanna turned to her partner. "Kristoff?"

Her partner smiled charmingly and took hold of the older woman's hand. "Shall we dance?"

Off they went. Shanna watched Kristoff handle Ali's mother with aplomb as he led her into a waltz. The problem was, with Kristoff engaged, well-wishers and competitors were headed her way.

Her father approached first with a proud gleam in his eyes and big hug. After she quickly introduced him to Ali and basked in her dad's pride, Shanna kissed his cheek. Then she grabbed Alejandro's hand and dragged him backstage, down a poorly lit, winding hallway, into an empty office. She had no idea who it belonged to—and didn't care—but she shut the door behind her and locked it.

"Hi." She smiled. "You came. Thank you."

God, could he hear her heart pounding like an up-tempo song at full blast?

"You sent tickets. This competition meant a great deal to you." Shanna heard the edge of anger in his voice, glimpsed it in his tight jaw.

"Not as much as I thought. I know that now, thanks to you." She bit her lip, wondering how bad it was going to hurt if he didn't want to hear what she had to say. "I'm sorry about...the other morning. You know, leaving you alone. For everything. Please tell me you don't hate me."

"I do not hate you."

His face still gave her no inkling about his true feelings, but Shanna considered not hating her a decent start. She rushed to Alejandro, threw her arms around his neck, and kissed him like there was no tomorrow.

Then again, unless she convinced him of her sincerity, there might not be a tomorrow for the two of them.

He kissed back. Oh, did he ever. And he tasted *so* good. Like brandy and a hint of cinnamon. Hot. And a few moments later, hungry, insistent as his mouth devoured hers. He threw his arms around her, banded them tight around her middle, as if telling her without words that she wasn't going anywhere again. She melted, might as well have become a puddle at his feet.

Long minutes and a pair of damp panties later, she broke away, breathing like she'd run a marathon. And unable to restrain a hopeful smile. "Does that mean you forgive me?"

"For leaving me in my own bed, alone? Hmm, I may need more... persuading." A smiled toyed at the corners of his lips.

"Does tonight work for you?" She cupped his cheek in her hand, looked right into those killer hazel eyes, and threw caution to the wind.

"I may require more nights. Many of them."

Hope burst in her heart, so explosive she could hardly breathe. "Ali, I am so sorry. What I did was insensitive. I know it. I knew it then. I was just...scared. But I'm not anymore. And I want you to know that I care about you. A lot."

He quirked a dark brow. "Care. In what way?"

Shanna knew she had his attention. Not only did she feel it against her hip, she felt it in his gaze, in the way his arms tightened around her.

"How much, *querida*?" he prompted again.

She swallowed down the tangle of anxiety and need and anticipation threatening to kill her courage. "I love you."

Those three words had barely cleared her lips before Ali stepped around her and, with an impatient arm, wiped every piece of paper off the flat, faux-wood desk and onto the floor. A moment later, her back was against the cool laminated surface and every inch of his body covered her completely, from the bunching shoulders beneath his elegant coat to the hard abs that rippled with every breath.

"Say it again." His voice was thick with demand.

"I love you."

"And you mean this?"

"Except my dad, I've never said those three words to a man. Ever."

Finally, expression warmed Alejandro's strong, square face. Happiness, hunger, adoration...love.

"*Te amo, querida.*" He dipped his head for a long, sweet kiss. "I love you, too."

Then he kissed her again, long endless moments where Shanna felt blissfully lost in passion. Alejandro's endless caress shimmered want in every crevice, corner, and nerve ending. She wanted the moment to last forever.

With a moan, he lifted his head, his hazel eyes snapping with a hunger like she'd never seen. "What I wish to do to you...with you, to show you how I feel... How do I get you out of this infernal costume so I can make love to you?"

"I want to," she breathed the words against his mouth. "I want that so much…but I was sewn into this costume. If you take it off, we won't get it back on, and I have nothing else to wear."

He cursed in Spanish, something that sounded melodious but was, no doubt, foul.

"I'll make it up to you."

He smiled, something sharp and greedy with his signature charm.

"We're leaving now. You will come to my bungalow and stay all night?"

"Yes." And the next, and the one after, and the one after that, if he'd have her.

"You will not leave?"

"In the morning? No."

"Ever?"

Was he saying… "Are you asking me to…move in with you?"

He clenched his jaw. "No."

Her stomach plummeted. "Of course not. I misunderstood."

"My *Mamá*, she would be very disappointed if we lived together. Just before you sent her to dance with Kristoff, a brilliant move, by the way, she asked if you were my girlfriend."

"You said yes." A smile crept across her mouth.

"I did, then I whispered in her ear. Do you recall?"

"Yes, what did you tell her? And what is a *nuera*?"

"I told her I had other plans." Alejandro grabbed her hand, kissed it, then whispered, "*Nuera* means daughter-in-law." He took a little black box from his pocket. "Interested in the role?"

Shock burst inside her, breath-catching and sweet. "You're proposing?"

"Yes."

"Aren't you supposed to be down on one knee?" she teased.

"I would rather be on top of you, always." He winked. "Will you marry me?"

"*YES!!!!*" She clutched Ali tight as he opened the box. She fell in love all over again. "Yes!"

"Good. I wasn't taking no for an answer."

"It's beautiful," she breathed as he stood up and slipped the square solitaire on her ring finger. Tears gathered in the corners of her eyes, slid down her cheeks. Probably ruining her mascara—and she didn't care. "When did you buy this?"

His cheeks flushed a dull red. "About four hours ago. But I have known that I love you for far longer than that."

"Me, too. I was just too afraid that love meant giving up my dream. I'm sorry. Never again."

"Together, we can face anything. Shall we tell my mother and your father?"

"Yes. Just... I want another moment alone with you." She squeezed his hand. "This is the happiest night of my life! The win, the engagement... Wow, almost too much good stuff to take in. I feel so complete."

He brought her against him for a lingering embrace. "Me, too. I will be here to share your triumphs for the rest of our lives. But..." he frowned. "What happened to the blackmailer? He threatened to circulate Kristoff's video to the judges to prevent you from competing and winning."

"I know. I've been scratching my head, too. Maybe he changed his mind?"

A pounding on the door interrupted their closeness and musings. Oops...someone wanted their office back, and they'd made an absolute mess.

Ali opened the door with an apology on his lips. "We are very sorry..."

But instead of an event manager standing on the other side, it was Kristoff.

"What?" Shanna asked. "Is something wrong?"

"I must talk to you."

She'd promised to talk to him in fifteen minutes. She supposed those were pretty much up. "Okay."

Kristoff paced; he looked oddly hesitant. "You are happy we won, yes?"

"Of course! Aren't you?"

He nodded. "Very."

"I don't know how, given your footage and the threat but—"

"I did that."

"Did what?"

Grimacing, he confessed, "I created the video. Before you force me from *Sneak Peek...*" He risked a glance at Ali. "The people in the video consented to be filmed. They are my...how should I say, boyfriend and girlfriend. We are together, and they agreed to help me."

Shanna had no idea Kristoff was in any sort of relationship, much less with both a man and a woman. Whatever floated his boat, but... "You're telling me you filmed the clip and left it for me with the black-mailing note? *You* staged this? Why the hell... I worried until I was sure I had no stomach left for days!"

"This, I know. I apologize. But, um...before I invest more years in being your partner, I must know if you will stay with me. If I pretended like the news of my relationship reached the judges, I wondered what would you do, keep me or dump me."

"So the blackmail...it wasn't real?"

"No." He grimaced. "Please do not hate me."

A moment of anger surged through her...then died. He would never have needed to test her if she hadn't spent years partner swap-ping to feed an ambition that, in the long run, had nearly consumed her spirit and happiness.

"I don't hate you. Just don't, um...surprise me again."

"Now I know where I stand, so...never." He snatched up her left hand, noted the ring there, and grabbed her in a bear hug. "Engaged? Congratulations! You are happy, yes?"

"Incredibly so." She sent Ali a warm smile, and he caressed her back in return.

"I think all will be good now," Kristoff pronounced.

"Not just good." Ali brought her closer to his side, and she rested her head on his shoulder. "It's going to be perfect. I'm going to be so happy."

"Are you sure?" Ali teased.

"I'm a champion with a great dance partner and a wonderfully hot fiancé. Oh, yeah." Shanna sent him a saucy smile of challenge. "Don't believe I'll be happy? Just watch me."

He slid his arms around her, and his kiss promised a passion that left her reeling. "Oh, I will."

Read on for more from Shayla Black!

Want a sexy office romance?
Read Naughty Little Secret.

Her boss. Her friend. Her secret lover?

NAUGHTY LITTLE SECRET
By Shayla Black
(available in eBook, print, and audio)

After divorcing her never-home husband, Lauren Southall plucked up her courage, dusted off her power suits, and returned to corporate life. Two years later, there's just one six-foot three, testosterone-packed problem: her ex-husband's good friend and her current boss, Noah Reeves. Lauren aches for him. But she can't possibly measure up to the silicone-packed professional cheerleaders he dates. So she hides her desire behind a professional persona and fantasizes.

For ten years, Noah Reeves has waited to make Lauren his. Once her divorce was final, he tracked down and hired the brilliant, dedicated woman. But when he's with her, it isn't spreadsheets and profit margins on his brain. Problem is, she's never seen him as anything but her ex-husband's pal. Now that she's finally a free woman and with him 40+ hours a week, well... he'd love to persuade her to throw in her nights and weekends. So Noah decides to romance her by day. By night, he becomes a mysterious stranger devoted only to her pleasure...and discovers she's hiding a naughty little secret of her own.

ABOUT SHAYLA BLACK

Shayla Black is the *New York Times* and *USA Today* bestselling author of more than seventy novels. For twenty years, she's written contemporary, erotic, paranormal, and historical romances via traditional, independent, foreign, and audio publishers. Her books have sold millions of copies and been published in a dozen languages.

Raised an only child, Shayla occupied herself with lots of daydreaming, much to the chagrin of her teachers. In college, she found her love for reading and realized that she could have a career publishing the stories spinning in her imagination. Though she graduated with a degree in Marketing/Advertising and embarked on a stint in corporate America to pay the bills, her heart has always been with her characters. She's thrilled that she's been living her dream as a fulltime author for the past eight years.

Shayla currently lives in North Texas with her wonderfully supportive husband, her daughter, and two spoiled tabbies. In her "free" time, she enjoys reality TV, reading, and listening to an eclectic blend of music.

Connect with me online:
    Website: http://shaylablack.com
    VIP Reader Newsletter: http://shayla.link/nwsltr
    Facebook Author Page: https://www.facebook.com/Shayla-BlackAuthor
    Facebook Book Beauties Chat Group: http://shayla.link/FBChat
    Instagram: https://instagram.com/ShaylaBlack/
    Twitter: http://twitter.com/Shayla_Black
    Amazon Author: http://shayla.link/AmazonFollow
    BookBub: http://shayla.link/BookBub
    Goodreads: http://shayla.link/goodreads
    YouTube: http://shayla.link/youtube

If you enjoyed this book, please review it or recommend it to others.

Keep in touch by engaging with me through one of the links above. Subscribe to my VIP Readers newsletter for exclusive excerpts and hang out in my Facebook Book Beauties group for live weekly #WineWednesday video chats full of fun, community, book chatter, and prizes. I love talking to readers!

MORE THAN WORDS

Contemporary romances that depict a love so complete, it can't be expressed with mere words.

DEVOTED LOVERS

Steamy, character-driven romantic suspenses about heroes who will do anything to love and protect the women bold enough to be theirs. Begins where Wicked Lovers ended.

WICKED LOVERS

Dark, dangerous, beyond-sexy romantic suspenses about high-octane men and the daring women they risk all for, even their hearts.

PERFECT GENTLEMEN

Suspenseful contemporary romances about the "Perfect Gentlemen" of Creighton Academy. Privileged, wealthy, and powerful friends—with a wild side.

MASTERS OF MÉNAGE

Very sexy romances about men of power and danger who share a kink—and a special woman. Though she's inexperienced, she isn't afraid to embrace all she desires.

SEXY CAPERS

Sassy, sinful contemporary romances with a pinch of suspense that show both the fun and angst of falling in love while snaring bad guys.

DOMS OF HER LIFE: RAINE FALLING

Super-sexy serialized contemporary romances about one tempestuous woman thoroughly in love with two friends and their battle to see who will ultimately win her heart.

DOMS OF HER LIFE: HEAVENLY RISING

Super-sexy serialized contemporary romances about one innocent and the two frenemies desperate to her touch, protect, and claim her as their own.

MISADVENTURES

Sexy, rompy standalone contemporary romances with a fun premise, fast pace, and high heat.

STANDALONES

Romances published independent of a series, some sexy, some sweet, all with a happy ending that's finished and complete.

HISTORICALS

Sexy stories about the bold rakes and audacious beauties of lush eras gone by.

PARANORMAL

Set in contemporary London, magic, myth, and emotions blend in the passionate, good-versus-evil Doomsday Brethren series.

—Join the—

ShaylaBLACK
NEW YORK TIMES AND USA TODAY BESTSELLING AUTHOR

Book Beauties
Facebook Group
http://shayla.link/FBChat

Join me for live,
interactive video chats
every #WineWednesday.
Be there for breaking
Shayla news, fun,
positive community,
giveaways, and more!

VIP Readers
NEWSLETTER
at ShaylaBlack.com

Be among the first to get
your greedy hands on
Shayla Black news, juicy
excerpts, cool VIP
giveaways—and more!

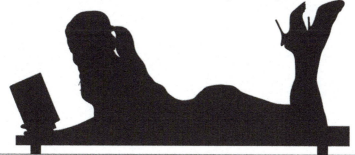

Made in the USA
Coppell, TX
01 September 2020